Cleopatra

The Mighty Warrior

Lorraine Rukarwa

pencil

ISBN 978-93-5667-097-6
© Lorraine Rukarwa 2022
Published in India 2022 by Pencil

A brand of
One Point Six Technologies Pvt. Ltd.
123, Building J2, Shram Seva Premises,
Wadala Truck Terminal, Wadala (E)
Mumbai 400037, Maharashtra, INDIA
E connect@thepencilapp.com
W www.thepencilapp.com

Author biography

Lorraine Rukarwa was born in Rusape Zimbabwe. She grew up in Msana Communal Lands in Mashonaland central Province. She is the eldest child in her family and was raised by her loving great grandmother. She is an author who likes to tell stories in a fictional manner. Cleopatra is her first book that she has published. She is a devoted Christian of the Roman catholic sect. She is a Disaster management specialist with a backgroung of Agriculture and Irrigation engineering. She loves to help people go through uncommunicated problems through writting.

CONTENTS

DIAGNOSIS 5

Uncle Mike 13

Budiriro 19

The Funeral 32

Francistown 38

Work 49

Bindura 54

Sangoma 57

Cleansing 66

Chinembiri 72

Stroke 85

Henry 91

Fibroids 96

Myomectomy 99

DIAGNOSIS

I felt as if I had been struck by a baboon clap when Sister Rachel told me the devastating result. For a moment my brain disc went blank and my body muscles all went numb, I did not think or feel anything. You could practically prick me with a needle and I could not feel any pain. I kept staring at the paper that I was given as if I was reading when in actual fact I was not even looking at the paper. No humanoid description can correctly comprehend the way that I was feeling at the time. My stomach began making sounds and I could feel sweat oozing out of my skin pores all over my body. Sister Rachel suddenly said,
"Do not go and kill yourself because of these results, it is not the end of the world". I managed to keep tears from flowing down my cheeks, I could not cry in front of the nurse lest I spend the next 30 minutes in the counselling ward.
"No, its ok sister it happens, there is no problem I will find a way out", I replied as I scratched my head with the long nails of my left hand that I fancy to keep long, suddenly the dandruff in my corn rows had started to itch. I gathered the remaining strength in my remaining working muscles, stood up and left the room without uttering any other word.
"Do not forget to take your flu medication", she said as I closed the door of the room. She must have said other

things but I did not hear it because I had now drowned deep in thoughts.

Normally, some women will cry uncontrollably in such situations, but I managed to walk away without shedding any tear or ask nagging questions to the health professional. Contrary to what I exhibited superficially, internally I was suffering and I was asking myself a lot of questions without any apparent answer. As I left the hospital, I forgot that there are taxis from Parirenyatwa hospital to the city centre. The diagnosis of an ovarian cancer was something that was never on my mind at this tender age. "Why had I gone for that pap smear in the first place?", I was beating myself. I was just 26 years, never had a baby, what was I doing in the oncology section after all. There is an African proverb that says "If you look for monkeys in the mountains you will definitely get to meet them. I had fetched monkeys in the mountains and I got to see them. Apparently, the hospital was offering free cervical cancer screening to all women for the period, so, I decided to try this free service which ended up giving me a free shock of my life. I should have stuck to my ordinary flu treatment and yellow fever vaccination that I had come for. Now I have to go back home with a heavy heart.

I carefully took the cycle track along Leopold Takawira street, I was avoiding using the busy tarred roadside because I knew that I was a moving statue and could get hit by a passing motorist. I was not myself anymore. All my dreams were shuttered in a flash, it felt as if the light of my life had been taken out all of a sudden. I was a health sensitive individual who exercised regularly and ate a healthy diet. I had a normal body mass index and was regularly checked for any communicable disease. I was an offspring and a descendant of patients of hypertension and diabetes, I was always checking myself lest I develop any of those conditions that troubles my mother and paternal grandmother. I had been taking good care of myself, that is why I had decided on this particular day to take the free service that was being offered by Parirenyatwa hospital. I had come also for a yellow fever vaccination prior to my planned trip to Tanzania in the coming months which I could not get after obtaining this shocking diagnosis. Many people were telling me about cheap clothes that I could buy and sell from Dar es Salaam. I needed to use the lumpsum gratuity that I had gotten from my previous job to start a clothing business and was contemplating on hoarding my goods from Tanzania. Tanzania is a country which has a high prevalence of dangerous variants of yellow fever and everyone who wants to visit the country should have been vaccinated against yellow fever.

I had dreamt of one day getting married and have my own family and the news had abruptly closed that chapter of my life. I carefully reflected on all my failed nuptial relationships. How I had kept myself pure until the time I reached 25. How I vehemently, denied my first love Edison from touching me all those years ago. Had I just given in I could be having a child about 8 years old now. I could recall the many times I kept those legs tightly crossed as I tried some romance with my college sweetheart Nigel to avoid any penetrative sex. I had always played it clean and kept myself for my husband on our wedding night.   Now, I will never have the privilege of becoming a mother in my life let alone live to see my friend's children get to high school. I saw myself as a case of lost hope, a futureless, childless and miserable human being who is just wasting oxygen on the planet earth. I remembered how my Aunt Teererai would be ridiculed by her in laws because she did not have a child. Teererai was the wife of my mother's brother Tinashe. She was a beautiful, well nurtured, hardworking and loving woman. She had never had chidren throughout her married life even a miscarriage. She had a rare condition of infertility. The family kept pressurizing Uncle Tinashe to marry another fruitful wife who would bear him children to carry the family name to the next generation. However, Uncle Tinashe had a daughter called Amara before marrying Teererai so he was satisfied with his loving wife. Teererai was affectionately known as Mai Amara which means mather of Amara and some people in the neighbourhood never knew that the girl was not her biological daughter. After all marriage is about husband and wife and children are just blessings from the union. The couple loved each other, they had achieved a lot of things together and they supported each other in every business enterprise they were doing. The couple had a fleet of buses and a chain of stores at Nyava Business Centre in Msana where Teererai was the overall financial manager. So Tinashe had loved her all in one wife, business partner, financial advisor and personal organiser.

The story of Aunt Teererai that I always saw and pitied on, was now going to happen to me.

Growing up I had crafted a life path that would take one step at a time until I achieve greatness. I had decided to take up the normal pathway to success, which requires a person to acquire a good education, get a good job, acquire a few necessities and eventually get married. I wanted to get into a marriage holding something in my hand and move away from the traditional way of getting into marriage with nothing and be treated like an asset that can be treated anyhow and discarded when its services are no longer required. The overrated marriage union always poses a lot of difficulty to the fairer sex if it allows the other sex to be too much in control. I wanted to be treated with respect and intergrity regardless of societal discernments. My vision was just darkened off like there was a power outage when one is watching a favourite soap opera. Everything was just taken off and I had no story to tell or no reason to live for the rest of my life. I had witnessed how woman suffer in marriages due to the fact that they are women. I recalled how my neighbours wife Lindiwe could be thrown out of the house by her husband Lloyd because of giving a chicken drumstick portion to a visiting friend. The woman gave a plate of Sadza and chicken to the visitor and mistakenly gave the visitor the drumstick. The woman was beaten up by the husband as if he was beating a stray dog. Lloyd could not show any remorse even if the wife is pregnant and lactating. On one occasion the Lindiwe fell on their sleeping two months old baby leading to the death of the child. The husband got away with murder because the family discouraged her from reporting the case to the police. The infant was secretly buried and it was case closed. The whole neighbourhood would stand still as Lloyd boasted about paying lobola of two cattle to the woman's family and claiming that he owned the woman as if she was some piece of property, it is probably one of the reasons that I remained unmarried until I become financially independent.

However, the economic situation in Zimbabwe deterred me from attaining these dreams that I had since I was a child. I had idolised my primary school headmistress at Gowa Primary school Mrs Matsika. The woman was virtually in control of everything around her from home to work. Her husband was an administrator in the department of roads but he could not make any decision before consulting his wife. All the school teachers at Gowa Primary school practically bowed down to her orders. I pictured myself with the same authority and independence so i would stop at nothing until I achieve my goals.

In 2006 the economy had practically crumbled down to the floor and everyone was thinking of leaving the country to look for greener pastures in other neighbouring countries. The thought of leaving the country had also struck me and I had done the paperwork to move to South Africa on a visitor's VISA for three months. I wanted to find out for myself if indeed there were abundant employment opportunities as portrayed by those people who would have moved there. I could envy my childhood friend Takudzwa who had moved to South Africa and was always telling me of many job opportunities available in the neighbouring country that I can grab with my qualifications and experience. Takudzwa would come home for Christmas with a double cab twin cab engraved with South African number plates dragging a full trailer of groceries that he would dish out to his kinsmen and friends. He would go buy beers for the entire neighbourhood while mingling with beautiful girls. It looked as if the grass is indeed greener on the other side. Takudzwa was just a qualified electrician and was managing such a lavish life. It is because of him that I wanted to give the neighbouring country a shot. For contingency purposes I had also decided to start a business of my own and live on the motherland nearer to my family and friends. I was slowly learning to cope with the prevailing economic hardships and now all of a sudden, I was in a situation that I did not know if there is any way out. "Why me?" I lamented as tears began flowing down my tiny cheeks. Since, I had a flu my temperature was a little higher than normal. I felt a breeze moving through my whole body as if I had just drank ice-cold water then it reaches an aching tooth.

My entire body developed some goose bumps an felt a sharp headache. Probably the fever had augmented due to too much stress on me at the moment. The nurse had given me a few painkillers and antibiotics but I was yet to take them so I reached out the pocket of my black jean skirt to take two of the paracetamols. I just swallowed them without any water, even the bitter taste of a pill could not be felt at that time. I was so in emotional pain that I could not feel any other pain or taste. The weather had changed and it was starting to rain. I had an umbrella on me but did not use it, I told myself to let it rain and wash away my pain. I did not feel any pain as the heavy drops of rain hit me in the face. My heart was in a lot of agony that I cannot clasp. If the thought of suicide had struck me then I would have easily taken poison. However, I was a person who always presented a good example to a lot of children and my decision was going to affect many people including the little girls of Denganyika village in Musana where I grew up. The girls probably were idolising me as an example of success to them. Many would have wanted to take my path. Little did they know that my path was full of rises and falls and other falls were too deep and too hard that it was not easy to get out. This type of fall is one such that those girls who idolized me would not be able to rise up from.

Uncle Mike

When the rain had stopped, I looked up with my clothes all soaked up. I began sneezing and as I reached out for my black purse to take a handkerchief, I saw a man wearing the camouflage army uniform who was just passing by. The man was tall and slim with the same stature as my uncle Mike.

"Bless you," he said to me as he passed by while I made a strong sneeze. "Thank you", I replied as I wiped my face with a white handkerchief that I was gifted by my mother when she came to visit me three years ago. Immediately, I got a flash of my favourite person who was not feeling well at the moment and admitted at Harare hospital. Uncle Mike was very ill and he was probably needing me the most and, there I was, crying over a diagnosis of my own.

I thought of going to Harare Hospital to see him and perhaps get some words of encouragement from him. He had been unwell for some time but was rushed to the hospital about 4 days ago after he had collapsed while taking a bath in his bathroom. Bernard who is his nephew whom he was staying with discovered him lying on the floor when he followed him to the toilet after realising that he had taken too long in the toilet. He then called an ambulance and went to the hospital where he was admitted to get hospital care. His vital signs were deteriorating every day. For instance the body temperature had remained too high, blood pressure was extremely low, blood sugar and oxygen levels were all too low, and so was the overall blood count so much that he needed an emergency blood transfusion. His blood group was rare and the national blood bank did not have his type at the moment, I was a match but my blood count results revealed that I too had a low blood count so it was not recommended for me to donate any blood. We were waiting for matching blood in the blood bank soon. The hospital had put him on oxygen while they ran several tests to ascertain the real cause of this system collapse. The poor man needed me more than I needed him. My clothes had dried up by the time I reached Copacabana bus terminus in downtown Harare. I boarded the next commuter omnibus to Highfields. I did not take the straight bus to the hospital since it was taking long to take off but I took a commuter omnibus bound for Highfields instead. I had to drop off at Southerton Police Station and walk all the way to Harare hospital. The man who had always had my back since I was a child was battling for his life. My history with him could fill a book. He was the one who went to pay lobola to my mother's family when my father had gotten my mother pregnant with me. We probably bonded when I was still in my mother's womb on that day. He took it upon himself to buy preparatory clothes for the pregnancy. He was so excited about my birth that he was the first to arrive at the Shamva mine Hospital the day I was born. He kept checking up on me and by the time I was 4 I began the transformation of loving him back and he overtook my father as the most important man and first love. He once had to almost go to jail for claiming that he was my father at a police roadblock. Although I would have answered that he is indeed my father, he failed to answer basic questions about me like how old I was, and what is my mother's name, because he had taken a few too many drinks and eventually that made the police suspicious. If it was not for my grandmother who came to the rescue, he would have been taken into police custody. Grandma had gone to buy some supplies at the Shamva bus terminus when the police came asking for the immunization status of children on the bus. Uncle Mike took it upon himself to answer the questions which he had no answers to.

This is the man who would support me even if I was wrong. He once stood by me when his sister Aunt Sandra accused me of stealing Mangoes from the next door at our rural home. As the woman furiously scolded me my uncle denied that I had done anything and the two siblings entered into a heated argument. I had indeed stolen the fruits but his defence made me stand by him and my aunt had to look stupid. He knew I had done it but he could not stand the site of me getting abused by any other person including his own sister, wife or even mother.

He was there lying in the hospital bed of ward B12 of Harare hospital or kuGomo as popularly known. He had sacrificed even his happiness for me and at one point he almost costed his marriage for my happiness. When I was doing my advanced level, he could fight with his wife for me to get to that level when his wife thought I should settle for a simple polytechnic course. The marriage was on the edge as he stood by me so that I could pursue my passion i really owed him one. I recall one day when I visited him in the company of his sister, he could find time to get to me and tell me exactly what was bothering him and ask for my opinion which he always trusted without any doubt. He could share with me virtually everything including his extramarital affairs and this was something I could keep to myself. He could tell me of his love child Russel whom he had with this woman when he had gone for an army retraining in Hwange in 1992.

He is the man who had showed me the capital city of Harare when I first come to town as an adolescent. He could show me how to switch on the television, how to go shopping and the art of buying around the top of the class shopping malls of Harare such as Sam Levy Village. He took me through the elevator and the escalator and he even introduced me to the banking system. I still remember how he could jokingly narrate the fear he saw in my eyes on the first ride in an elevator. He could usher me through all the entertainment arenas of Harare like the Harare showgrounds for me to see the fireworks display during the Agricultural show week. He once took me to the lunar park and paid for my maiden ride of the big wheel, at one point he took me to the National sports stadium to watch the football match between Dynamos and Black Rhinos when he had two tickets from his work. Uncle Mike was a father, friend and brother at the same time to me. He was so bent on seeing me enjoy my youth and not having another strange man take advantage of me through the same things that he could do himself. He wanted me to be on top of the current affairs of the country so that I will not be lied to by politicians, he could buy the daily Herald and ask me to read the stories in it then ask me every day what stories were in the paper, that way I was forced to read the paper and at least watch the news to avoid embarrassment when asked. When I reached Harare Hospital entrance, my tears dried up as I prepared to see him. I did not want him to notice my troubled face lest he become even more worried in his condition. The results of my diagnosis were probably ill timed. Maybe I should have taken one problem at a time. I was supposed to wait for my uncle to recover before I opened a can of worms for myself. I never for once expected those kinds of results which is why a reluctantly took the test.

Uncle Mike was lying on the bed and the fruit basket that we had brought the previous day was still there on the table untouched. My heart went down as I saw his pale looking face and unimproved condition from the previous day. He opened his eyes and forced a smile. I could feel he was in much pain. I began to play the memories of the happy moments that we had together. The open and prize giving day for my school when I was in form 3, when I scooped the most prizes including the overall best student. I was also the best in three subjects viz Mathematics, Accounting and Physical science, and was the best in sports and I scooped an additional prize on leadership. This day I saw my Uncle feeling proud of me, picking me up and raising me high like he raised me when I was just a toddler. He once raised me up so that I could see the masquerades dance on Independence Day at Shamva gold mine when I was still too short to see anything. The surprise birthday party he did for me on my 21st birthday when he bought me a cake, made a small celebration for the day. He could proudly wear the clothes that I had bought him using my first salaries. The clothes were not as expensive as what he had in his wardrobe but he adored them. The way he rushed to Westend clinic the day I got sick from malaria when I was doing temporary teaching in

Guruve during my gap year after I finished high school. The way he stopped everything he was doing in order to take me to the airport on my first international flight on an educational trip to Pretoria when I was working for Agrihad. A lot of such memories could just flow into my brain as I looked at my ailing uncle. We still had a lot of unfinished business I thought as I smiled back at him. He had something to tell me but he was interrupted by his sister in law Bertha who came in and began to talk to him. Bertha was the sister to his late wife Winnie. She was the one staying with his ten year old daughter Jasmine. She could not come with the girl due to the hospital regulations which forbid minors from visiting sick relatives. Jasmine remained at home in Glen Norah and aunt Bertha would take a picture of Uncle Mike and record a small video of him on her phone to show to her. We persuaded him to try and eat and he eventually finished one banana and a tub of yoghurt. My heart melted as I remembered how much my Uncle adored his food. I managed to hold my composure as I stared at him trying to drink water from a bottle while shivering. The man who once loved his food can now struggle to finish a small tub of yoghurt and a banana. I would have cried but I did not want him to feel bad about the situation. I wanted to continue giving him hope for life and a reason to keep fighting.

Budiriro

From the Hospital I boarded a bus and went to Budiriro where I was staying with my grand aunt Agnes. Agnes was grandmother's niece. She was the daughter of my grandmothers' brother. Aunt Agnes had always adored my hardwork since I was a child and was prepared to show me the other side of life. The life of a hardworking woman. She would call me to stay with her kids each time she went to South Africa ever since I was a teenager. Now that all her children were grown up and have settled for work elsewhere in the world. She could rely on me to keep her house in shape. I had recently, lost my job from Agrihad enterprises, a company where I was working due to company closure. The company had faced liquidation due to the prevailing economic situation in the country. The Netherlands based shareholders had decided to liquidate the company since it was no longer profitable. I had decided to stay with her so that I could copy some notes about life. She is the one who was mentoring me and had helped me in processing the papers to move to South Africa. On this particular day she had travelled to South Africa and I was on my own for the next 10 days. Aunty Agnes was a cross boarder trader who had earned a living through selling seat covers and other household embroidery to her customers in Bloemfontein South Africa. She would travel to South Africa for two weeks that run to the end of each month to sell her staff and also collect money from the credit customers. The few moment that I was with my uncle had brought a little healing to my soul and has taken my thought off my own problems. Uncle was in great pain and I thought it was time to pray for his total healing. He is not in the best hands, I thought to myself. If I had money, he could have been admitted in a top of the class hospital receiving the best care money can buy. I had to keep trying hard in life in order to reach that level but in the meantime all my efforts were in vain. I had been practically reduced to an educated beggar myself due to the prevailing high inflation economy. I could not afford to buy myself sanitary wear and had reverted back to the traditional cloth which was not safe for my compromised health. The gratuity that I got from Agrihad was losing value each day and the three years I had worked for this company was not going to have anything that I could hold to remember for it except for a poor quality two plate stove which was nicknamed "mukadzi usaende" which means "My wife do not go" since it was common with the newly married wives.

I opened the door and sat on the sofa wondering where to start. I had sat down for less than three minutes when I had a knock on the door. I replied and I tried to open the door and Maggie barged in hurriedly. Before I could say anything, I realized five of her friends had surrounded my door in a horse shoe formation. " Is everything ok", I asked as I sensed some tension.

"Tell us you cheap whore what are you doing with my boyfriend", uttered Maggie furiously. I looked at her face and yes, she was talking to me with so much rage, her eyes were hot red like an angry Jaguar. I realized that these people were not playing with me.

"What do you mean Maggie, I do not know anything", before I could finish my statement Maggie had raised her hand in order to slap me right in the face. I blocked it with my hand, the other girls mistook it for an attack on their friend so they all closed in on me. They wanted to watch as I got hit and not the other way round. I pushed them all leaving two of them down on the floor. Maggie slapped me on the back as I jumped out of the door and ran into the Landlord's house.

"What is wrong", Tanya the Landlady asked with much amusement on her face. Tanya was relaxing on the sofa of her lounge while she watched 4 o'clock News on her 16-inch colour TV. She was alone, her kids were still in school or probably on their way back.

Madam Landlady had noticed something amiss about the speed I used to enter her sitting room, closed the door behind me and my continued panting in anger and disbelief.

All because of a mere gossip about a man Maggie had forgotten all the good deeds that I had done for her. Maggie once had a complicated abortion attempt and had no money to get specialist treatment and I led a go fund campaign for her hospital fees. She had gotten pregnant to a one night stand man who was a truck driver in transit to Tanzania and had not taken any details of the man such as the name and origin. She discovered a month later that she was pregnant and had no option than try to terminate the pregnancy. She consulted a herbalist who gave her some herbs that she took. The result was a painful experience that she cried like a child with her body now pale like a scone. I felt for her and immediately took her to Harare

Hospital to get treatment using my own money. I got her admitted and she finally had the successful abortion at Harare hospital but the hospital bill was so high that she could not afford. I therefore led a campaign to source money from people to raise money for the bill. This is how she decided to pay me back I lamented whilst looking at her hands which were now shivering in anger. Even her friend had thrown all the good deeds I had done for them too out of the window and had chosen to confront me over a man. I never leave a friend in a situation and would do whatever it takes to restore their problem no matter what kind of problems they present to me, ranging from relationship, mental, physical health and even spiritual problems. I am a gifted natural counsellor who is able to talk to anyone in any situation. People are so quick to forget the good sacrifices that we make for them. I once faced the same situation when I was working for Agrihad. I used to work with Prisca who was the administration assistant. Prisca was a selfish person who wanted everything good to be associated with her these include good people, good decisions and successful results. It was her hunger for prosperity that led them into a hell of a life. She joined Agrihad as an intern just two months after her graduation at Trust Academy in Harare. Joining this organisation was quite a remarkable achievement for her. She was the only one in her family who had gone to this level. Things were moving well for her since she was considered to be the pioneer of the organisation. The company had considered her to be cheap labour as she never complained and was a yes man who agreed to anything the Boss Den told her. She practically worshipped Boss Den and would take everything he had said as a commandment. Her behaviour made her the boss's confidante and informant. I had tried to be her friend but all my efforts were in vain. At one point we ate from the same plate. I was trying to build a lasting relationship with her. However, the moment that she suspected for some reason that I was having an affair with her married boyfriend Calvin she had to bite me in the back. She was so in love with this guy that she ignored her own mother's plea to sit down with her and discuss matters that were at her heart. She never wanted anyone to get between her and this man that she had to see off her best friend who had come for a sleep over a few hours into her arrival just to be with her man.

This lady actually connived with the management to have me fired. She forgot all the sacrifices I made for her. Apparently, she was too jealous of my friendship with her boyfriend whom I treated as an elder brother. The guy could give me constructive advice about how to deal with life situations. Apparently, Calvin was not keen to divorce his wife and was willing to take Prisca as his second wife or rather make her remain his side chick and would relate to her as an employment benefit. I nearly took a beating from his wife because she thought I was not advising my brother as I should have done. One day I had gone to the office to do some reports in the office, coincidentally he too was having to do some report and it began to rain. Everyone had gone home except the two of us. We then drove home after the 45-minute rain at about 8 o'clock. Prisca got furious and although she directed her anger at her boyfriend I discovered for once that she did not trust me. She could do anything for this man including conniving with the human resources department to get me fired and thus eliminating me from the picture. I could not even get the chance to explain that we were working in different offices until the time to go when he had shouted for me to pack up and go.

"These girls want to attack me", I answered my land lady as she tried to open the door. The girls were now at the door and barking like dogs.

"Stop it you ladies, this is my house, do you not have any respect", shouted landlady onto the angry group.

"Let her come out Mama we want to teach her a lesson that she will never forget", they replied with their voice's full of fury. To my surprise one of the girls was the alleged man's sister. Gertrude was the sister to Tawanda who is Maggi's boyfriend. How could someone fight a Brother's mistress. What if Tawanda was my boyfriend too and choose to marry me instead of Maggie', what kind of family will it become. It's a thought that just struck me. It once happened to my Aunt Agnes when she married the father of her children. The sister of the husband did not like her but would prefer her best friend Beauty to marry her brother. Eventually, the brother chose Agnes over her friend. The sister took years to apologise and mend her relationship. Had she kept her choices to herself then she would not have to go through so much in her life.

"Honestly, Mother I did not have anything to do with her man she is lying", I shouted from the landlady's seating room.

"Hey, do you think we are all fools, come out here and say those things to our faces", they shouted from outside. At this point I realized that my words will anger the mob even more so I decided to keep quiet and let madam Land lady handle the situation her way.

The land lady closed the door and instructed me to sit down. The posse was taken behind the house. I was praying they would disperse before it becomes a public fight lest the police arrest us and I end up paying a fine which I cannot afford. My image was tarnished in the society already, I would not need evidence of a fine ticket. The police are also human and they will judge me and consider Maggie's allegations to be true and I was going to be branded a partner snatcher by the entire neighbourhood. It once happened to my friend Bella in Guruve when we were doing our temporary teaching when the wife of a fellow teacher from the school accused her of having an affair with her husband. The wife hired a bouncer to attack Bella. My friend Bella was beaten up and had bruises all over her body. I took her to the nearest police post to report the case and only to look stupid in front of the police who directed the blame on Bella no matter how hard she tried to explain her situation. I realised that society and even police does not take the side of the accused woman and they further humiliate the woman. Bella cried all the way to the hospital to get treatment and even some of the health personnel looked at her in shame as they attended to her. Only the headmaster took time to listen to her side of the story and recommended for the teacher to be transferred from the school because of the violent behaviour his wife had exhibited. However, she had to go to college after the tenure of her temporary teaching contract and start a new life. Bella is now married but she always narrates this story whenever we meet or chat on social media. It was a memorable scary situation that I did not want to find myself in no matter what. I looked through the window as the girls opened the gate to leave the premises while still shouting some vulgar words and referring to my name. A sigh of relief got into me when the Land lady came in and told me that it was now safe to go to my house. She did not ask for any explanation, so it was another reprieve for me. I did not want to explain my innocence to anyone because no one would dare to listen. Maybe the land lady had understood my situation. She was staying with her two sons Tanaka 16 and Tavonga 14 who were in secondary school and have been a widow since Tanaka the eldest of them was ten and did not decide to remarry because of reasons best known to herself.

Chapter 4 Budiriro 2

The news of the confrontation spread across the neighbourhood. The first person to come to see me was Stewart who happened to be my ex-boyfriend. The guy was bitter after our recent breakup that I never expected any consolation from him.

"Hey, I heard that they attacked you", he started.

"Yes', I replied eagerly waiting for the next bombshell.

"It's saves you right, but Cleopatra why did you go telling people that I have a small blamby and could not satisfy you was breaking up with me not enough", he said to me angrily

I just nodded my head in extreme anger I would have hit him with a hammer. I controlled myself then turned around and got back into the gate without answering any word lest I create another drama. But surely who was spreading that nasty rumour. I never discuss bedroom stories with anyone. Stewart had every reason to be angry but now is not the time to get worked out. There is a fresh story brewing on me. He should have waited for another day to ask me this story.

"You cheap whore, they should have killed you', he continued as I moved away from him.

Little did I know that there were a lot a people who watched the confrontation. Stewart and I dated for the past 3 weeks and I broke up with him after realizing that he was not my type. Steward was an old-fashioned person who regarded a woman as an object of sexual pleasure and never respected my feelings. I usually do not argue with man of such calibre but I just leave them alone. I do not want to be slave to my lover that is why I terminate the relationship before it gets deeper. I had watched as my Cousin Jillian always came home to see grandmother after serious abuses by her husband. Jillian would come from the in-laws in the middle of the night after she would have been fatally assaulted by her unwed husband in the full view of her in laws. It is because of the intervention of uncle Mike that the husband stopped any abuse of her. Uncle Mike had to go and threaten him using his army antics. I did not want to see myself in an abusive relationship of my own so I needed to cut it short before anyone gets hurt. However, Steward did not take the break up easily that is why he rejoiced in my disgrace. I thought for once that he was the mastermind of this whole fiasco.

"Why did he do that?", I kept asking myself the question with no apparent riposte. So how can he turn the entire neighbourhood against me in a twinkle of an eye.

Just as I was lamenting on what had just happened, I had another knock on my door. This time it was Patrick, who is Aunt Agnes's cousin. I was so happy that it was not Stewart who had followed me or else I would have been pushed to the limit. Patrick, and his new wife used to keep meat portions in Aunty Agnes's refrigerator so I thought he had come to collect one. Apparently, he had heard the news of the confrontation and wanted to hear from me first hand.

"So, tell me Cleo, what happened, are you actually sleeping with Maggie's man, what do you girls see in that dump-head?", he asked.

"Patrick let me tell you the truth, I do not know where this is coming from, you can even ask the guy if he knows me, I surely do not know where this is coming from", I replied.

"That is what I want to know because I never saw you with him unless you meet behind our back. Anything is possible because you are grownups", he responded.

This statement showed me that I was wasting my time explaining anything, Patrick had chosen to believe the rest of the people. It was something that was going around town without my knowledge. Therefore, when Tawanda visited my house about 3 days ago when he wanted to see aunty Agnes. People concluded that he had come to see me and that we probably slept together. Some people cannot believe that two people of opposite sex can be together in one room and not sleep together. On that particular day he was watching the unfolding news of the defeat of Manchester united to Everton Fc on television. He was even calling his friend who supported Manchester united and informing them about their team's loss. He stayed for about 30 minutes and then left. That is the only time me and Tawanda has ever had a close interaction. For anyone to think that I was in love with him was ridiculous, we do not even talk and when we cross each other on the pathway we only wave at each other. This absurd allegation was something else I wondered as I tried to digest the words of Patrick. I stared at him and saw his face full of disbelief. I was about to burst out and tell him to back off, mind his own business and leave me alone when his heavily pregnant wife Angela showed up and looked at me again with so much rage. She threw a plastic bag on me and said,

'Cleo give me a packet of beef, you cheap slut you never learn.", she told me angrily.

I did not ask anything I just got into the house and brought a packet of beef and handed it over to her. For the second time in less than 24hours I have been accused of infidelity with people's man. What exactly is the meaning of this I asked myself? This day should be deleted from the calendar because it has too much to remember, a lot had happened to me for the day. I needed a break. I always require time to meditate on my life before making any decision.

"You have no shame, now you finished with Maggie's man and now you want mine, hehehe my friend I am the daughter of a Sangoma I will sort you and make white ants ooze out of your private part if you play with my man. ', she shouted as she took the packet of meat out of my hand and pulled her husband away by dragging him like she is dragging a toddler who is refusing to bath. Angela too was quick to forget the good things I had done to her. When she eloped to Patrick everyone in aunt Agnes's family did not like her because they thought that Patrick is not the one who had gotten her pregnant. Angela was dating two guys when she got pregnant and she had chosen to elope to Patrick who was the quietest and so in love. There was highest chance that the pregnancy belonged to the other guy. Patrick had only come to

Budiriro from Gweru where he was working every month end compared to the other boyfriend who was staying in the hood. The family was eagerly waiting from the baby to be born in the next two months as she claimed but the pregnancy looked so ripe it would paturate in the next 3 days. Angela only wanted to take it on me so that is she feels any labour pain she would accuse me of causing so much stress on her.

I immediately closed my ears and did not want to take more insults and got back into the house.

'What is happening to me?', I cried and all the tears began to fall out of me. The tears I had withheld after the medical diagnosis, the tears of seeing my ailing uncle and the tears of enduring insults from Maggie and her friends, the insults from Stewart and the humiliation from Patrick's wife. What could be the meaning of this predicament. I cried until I felt a cramp in my chest and tears could not flow anymore.

While I was crying, I received a phone call from a stranger. It was a private number so I answered.

It was an unfamiliar voice on the other end.

"Hello you cheap whore i would ask you to leave my husband if you want to walk freely in the streets of Budiriro.

"Sorry who is this madam I do not know you and who is your husband"

Surely this is not happening to me again. I thought to myself.   .

I just cut the call off and put my phone on silent lest this mad woman continue to pester me. A few moments later she sent a short message telling me her piece of mind I then realised the number belonged to Martha. Martha the wife of Mr Nenguwo the mechanic. Apparently, this man was having an affair with my namesake Cleopatra Nyamayaro. Martha must have heard of Maggies story and thought that I was the one having an affair with her husband. It never rains but it pours I said to myself as I read the long message on my phone. She had exhausted all the space on the phone telling me her mind. I was not moved by the words. I had more people wanting to pull out my throat I could not be moved by such a shenanigan. I meditated as I lay on the sofa of my Auntie Agnes's sitting room and eventually fell asleep

The Funeral

I do not know how I fell asleep I was woken up by a phone call from my phone at around 2 am. It was my aunt Bertha on the phone. She had just been called by Harare Hospital and told that Uncle Mike was no more. I froze to the core, I stopped thinking, I did not know what to say to her.

"Just stay strong Cleo, it is the God's way, we all will leave this earth one day, your uncle had just led the way he is gone before us and we will meet him one day", she continued.

I just dropped the phone and started to move up and down the house hopelessly. If I had cried loudly, I would have woken up the landlord and probably burden her again with my problem. I eventually sat down on the stool and began asking myself why. Tears began to flow down my cheeks. I tried to make a cup of coffee but it did not stop the tears from flowing down. I drank cold water and still it did not help. I was really going to live this life alone henceforth. The man who had helped mould me into this person that I am today was no longer breathing and I was not going to see him again. The whole of his life and stories he told me was all going to be history.

I eventually gathered my serenity and began calling and texting all relatives in my phone contact register and telling them about the development. I thought of how my grandmother would feel upon learning of her son's death. The poor lady was practically living this life for her son and his departure could be so devastating. The last time I saw my grandma in so much pain was when she lost my father. The woman could not hide her pain as she buried her eldest son she had also buried her only daughter Sandra. Now she was going to bury her remaining son. And the hope of the next generation has been shattered on me too. It's hard for a mother to bury all her children and Grandma was going to be in unbelievable pain. She is the person whom I was feeling for more than myself, My father had other 3 children Munyaradzi, Farai and Tatenda from his second marriage. Her late daughter had left two sons Ryan and Aiden who are now based in South Africa and these were not so close to her. It means that he only had me and probably Jasmine as her children. She was witnessing as her family line get cut off from the second level while she remained at the top. I had lost a father and confidant and he had died before I shared with him my problems. Maybe he could have given me advise, strength and encouragement to live.

All these things that had happened to me yesterday was a precursor to the more devastating news that I was going to hear. Suddenly, I started believing in the superstition that one is bound to experience bad luck when a person so close to them is about to die. It was evident that these ancestors were not so wrong after all. I began to believe in the African culture from this day onwards.

I took the first taxi to Highfields for the funeral arrangements with the other senior members of the family. We started by taking the furniture out so that we create space for the guest to gather. It was not long when the daughters in law of the family arrived and I joined the other group of relatives who went to Harare hospital to arrange for the repatriation of the body. My uncle's body was handed over to Doves funeral parlour .The army decided to take over the funeral from then on. The body was taken to the rural home so that it will lie in state for burial the next day.

When the motorcade carrying my uncle's, body reached the rural home. I could not hold my tears as I saw my grandmother crying uncontrollably as they carried the coffin into the round hut. It was indeed the last vigil that we spend with my uncle. The roman catholic congregants of St Thomas Catholic Church took over and said some prayers before letting the relatives and mourners start with their song and dance. I was there sitting in a corner with other people I did not get a wink of sleep until the next morning. I am one person who does not sleep during gatherings. Since I was a child, I did not sleep at my grandfather's memorial when I was still 5 years old so much that all the relatives were surprised but let's say I am a night owl. The next morning saw the church preparing for a church mass for my uncle. I was just sitting there were family friends who were doing some acts to relive the life of my uncle. Speaker after speaker they lamented on the kindness and sweet life that my uncle had lived all the 50 years of his life.

I looked helpless as the 6 soldiers carried the coffin from the house to the burial place. Uncle had always wanted to be buried in the family graveyard next to his father's grave. The elders had granted him his wish and pegged the grave just beneath his father's grave. Grand pa had died when I was 5 years old. I never got to meet him because he died when I was still an infant. The people who lived with him always narrated how this man adored his sons. He was a patriarch who did not value his only daughter Sandra. He believed that women are just objects and cannot be part of the decision-making process in the family. Maybe he would have changed his mind if he had lived to see me climbing my ladder of success against all odds.

They put the coffin down awaiting the catholic priest to finish his prayers and then they finish with the gun salute for the departed soldier who had served for the national army throughout his working career. This was the only honour that the government could give him since it had failed him economically.

The man who was once the bread winner and force to reckon with in the entire clan was earning enough money to buy one united states dollar per month. The money he had to queue for hours in order to get. The economy had gone down to the ground and the value of the dollar was crumbling down each night. People had to queue up for virtually everything including the toilet paper. The average Zimbabwean person was emaciated meaning that they were weighing less than 50kg and you could hardly find an obese person in the streets except for children of drivers. Yes, drivers and security guards had become the most important people in the economy. The driver would accept negotiation if you want to travel from one point to another and the security guard would be paid by people who would want a favour to be first in a long queue for the shop which he works. My uncle had to adopt from his luxurious life that he was used to and start running around to put food in his mouth. He was divorced from his wife Chipo who had grown a mental problem and his only child

Jasmine was staying with his late wife Winnie's sister Bertha. As a result, he had to take down his stresses on his own or rely on low quality and homemade opaque beer that was being sold illegally in the neighbourhood. He was a chain smoker and had to rely on rejected tobacco stolen from auction floors which he would mix with a little processed Madison cigarette. I believe that adjusting to the situation in the country was not easy for my uncle that is why his body gave in to infections easily which eventually led to his demise. Although, he had an illness I would want to believe that the economic situation in the country had killed him more than the disease itself. I watched the proceedings in tears as they lowered the coffin into the grave and used big boulders to do whatever they were doing in the name of burial. It was indeed the end of Uncle Mike, we were never going to see him again. He had died before I could spoil him as I had always wished. With my situation it is not long until I join the rest of my kinsmen in this sacred spot of the 5-hectare rural plot. "Life goes on" I told myself internally as I walked back to the house for final rites and distribution of estate. My uncle's clothes were put under a tree and sprinkled with holy water for them to be shared among his remaining relatives as per the cultural norm and it was indeed the end of my uncle. The man had finished his race and the honours was upon us the remaining ones to keep his legacy alive and live our own regardless of where destiny takes us. It was time for me to get back to basics and think of my own problems. One by one all the people who had come for the funeral began to disburse and it was only the family members who remained behind so that we conduct the morning ritual the next morning as per cultural norm. In our culture early morning after burying an adult you go to the grave and see if the grave has not been tempered with. Should you find suspicious footprints on the grave then the family will consult a traditional healer who will tell them if anyone had tempered with the grave and ensure that necessary steps are taken to avoid further harm to the surviving family members.

Francistown

Three days after the burial of my uncle I got back to Budiriro and I met my aunt Agnes there, she had just returned from South Africa upon hearing the news of Uncle Mike passing. However , she could not arrive in time for the funeral and she had just landed this morning with the first Intercape bus that touches down Harare's roadport as early as 6 am. The funeral was so hectic for me so I decided to sleep on the floor to get enough rest. I was not in a condition to tell her about anything that happened in her absence. My flue had subsided on its own due to so much stress but I had to keep taking my antibiotic course to avoid developing a resistance to antibiotics. Auntie Agnes might have heard what had happened to me because as I was winking off to sleep, I heard her say that

"It happens each time someone close to you is about to die, you come across these trials and tribulations, I lost 200 dollars to crooks the day my mother died".

I continued to sleep pretending as if I was not hearing anything, she might have thought I was already sleeping when she suddenly stopped talking. I knew she wanted to tell me how she was crooked by conmen in the downtown of Harare, the day she lost her mother. The man pretended to be salesman who can get those shoes at a lower price than the one on the display. She was made to believe their lies and gave them the money for two pairs and they went into the shop and never returned with the shoes. That is when she looked up and saw a big sign clearly written, BEWARE OF CONMEN WE DO NOT HAVE SALESMAN OUTSIDE THE SHOP. She had to walk on foot all the way to Harare hospital in confusion and only to find her mother's body transferred to the mortuary.

When I woke up the next morning, I realised that I needed to woman up and get on my feet. Life henceforth was going to be lonely. I decided to go to Botswana and buy some items for consumption and resale any surplus. The trip will give me an idea of which business enterprize to venture into. After getting blessings from Auntie Agnes I packed my bag and embarked on a 24hour journey to Francistown by train. I was full of excitement as I boarded the 8pm train to Bulawayo. I was so full of exhilaration when I heard a loud hoot as the locomotive took off for Bulawayo. I was waiting for it to increase its speed but it kept at that slow pace. The vehicle stopped at every station and only got to Gweru early in the morning. The vendors kept doing rounds in the train as they tried to catch impromptu buyers aboard the train. I nearly bought some fried fish in Norton because it was smelling so good and appetising. It was my first time to get on a train. I had not bought the ticket in advance so I waited for the conductor to come. I sat next to a couple who was going to Chegutu them too had not paid for their tickets. However, when the conductor came the couple disappeared only to return when the conductor had already passed. They kept dodging the conductor until they got off in Chegutu, I saw how people were risking their lives for a free train ride. At around midday we reached the Bulawayo train station and found the Francistown train waiting for us. There was no time to buy any food I just had to jump on the train which was so ready to take off. The train took off at exactly 1230hours and it had delayed because of the Harare-Bulawayo train. The vehicle cruised past the plain land of Matebeleland and before we knew it we were in Plumtree. The customs people had already made rounds in the train and clearing our passage into the neighbouring country. We made a brief stop at the border post as we waited for a few passengers to pay duty for their goods. I felt a difference in the two journeys by train since the other one was slow as a snail and the other one was a fast-paced train. Our country's transport system was so in the old age. Even the ticket system was poor. A lot of people had a free journey to Bulawayo because they managed to dodge the conductor. The bar area in the Botswana train was well stocked and full of cold drinks and snacks you could hardly see a vendor selling stuff in the train. Language barrier was beginning to take shape as the train was full of people from diverse backgrounds ranging from Ndebele, Shona, Tonga, Venda and Tswana. It was my first time to be in a place so rich and diverse.

I was so amused of the transition of the veld from the Savannah to the semi desert vegetation in Botswana. The beautiful semi desert grassland took my attention to the extent that I did not notice how the train reached Francistown at around 7pm. I had asked the woman sitting on an adjacent seat how I could get cheap overnight accommodation in the town. The well-lit border town looked beautiful in the night I could not wait to explore it the next morning. The lady told me to follow her because she knew of a place where we can get cheap overnight shelter. I just needed somewhere to lay my head and be able to freshen up in the morning. The train station was a non-starter since the Botswana police would arrest anyone caught loitering or sleeping around the train station at around midnight when all the trains would have docked. I followed my newly found friend whom I did not ask her name. We paid 10 pula for a taxi to go to the nearest suburb. Apparently, this woman was a cross boarder trader who used to hoard groceries for resale in Zimbabwe. It was a lucrative business venture as she narrated how much profit she was making for every trip. She could make 2 or three trips per month and was making a fortune. I was almost tempted to join her business venture but had to stick to my maiden shopping spree as planned. During this trip to the suburb I was so composed and thinking of how lucky I was to bump into this business minded woman. Unfortunately, she was not going shopping the next day since she wanted to see some of her customers and then go back to Zimbabwe in two days. She had smuggled Zimbabwean cigarettes and some traditional herbs that she was going to sell to Zimbabweans based in Francistown. Throughout the 10-minute drive she had told me enough to lure me into joining her business. We were taken to a house and paid our 20 pula each for accommodation. We were ushered to the house full of other ladies. It was so full a house that we had to squeeze in a little corner. I was surprised to see how my sisters were doing in the foreign land. Most of the girls were living there for over nine months and had to put up like that every day. Quite a number of them were now into prostitution and surprisingly even the woman who had come with me was also into prostitution she actually sneaked out to see a man and never returned that night. I held my tears as I noticed how much the economic condition had made our very own daughters destitute in this foreign land. I could think of their parents who gladly receive groceries from these girls and brag about it at church gatherings. Anyone would cry at the sight of this situation.

I was so tired of the train journey that I just removed my shoes and secured my money in my underpants pocket and winked off to sleep. I woke up, brushed my teeth and took off for my shopping in the city of Francistown. The sight of a lot of man and the bus stop also puzzled me. Then suddenly a car that was driven by a white man stopped. He wanted 5 strong guys to work at his farm and give them 50 pula each for the day. The men rushed to the vehicle in so much pressure that it was difficult to get to the top five. He eventually took ten of them and went off. I wondered what if this man was into human trafficking, it was a dangerous and risky situation our brothers had to go through. I was surprised also to see how sons of the soil are toiling in the neighbouring countries. I was so dismayed that I never envied Takudzwa again. I told myself that I need to go back home. It was clear that the grass is not greener on the other side. We just needed to water our grass and make it greener.

I started with my shopping spree in Francistown. At first it was still morning so I did not need to follow the horde to cheap wholesalers and Chinese owned shops. There I witness how women from my country were stealing clothes and several items from Chinese owned shops. It seemed that was another cash avenue for these foreigners. It means that some of these people we were envying were actually shop lifters in the foreign nation. I finished my shopping before 3pm so I decided to take a bus to Bulawayo instead, of the train lest I take the whole week on the road. I also wanted to experience the bus ride.

I took one cart pusher to push my luggage from the city to the bus station. As we moved toward the secluded area, I noticed 4 more man following. Immediately my heart began to pound. I could not say anything as I hoped behind the cartman.

"Hey you stop,' one of the men shouted, it was a man in his twenties and he looked wasted.

We stopped the cart and listen to what he had to ask.

"My sister you cannot go with those pulas give them to us", he shouted angrily.

I sensed danger as it appeared that the cartman and these thieves knew each other meaning that I was on my own and in danger. My own people had become robbers in the neighbouring country and they were robbing their own. I beat myself for not going back to the train.

"I realised that they were speaking my language so I answered them in my language and told them to at least have pity on me. They knew the situation back home and they surely cannot do that to their sister. I was so calm as I negotiated with them. I was actually negotiating to give my own money to thieves it was unbelievable.

"Is she trying to be difficult', said the bouncer of them all as he tried to reach out of his pocket", he must have been looking for a weapon to scare me with. I raised my hand to stop him, I looked at them all in the face, smiled and reached for my pocket and gave them all the money that was in there.

"ok, guys let us pass you can have this and buy yourself some drinks", I said to them as if I was giving money to my friend. A Policeman passing by must have thought that we are in good books. I did not shout or do anything but just complied with them for my own safety.

One of them then said

"Let's go guys, she is our sister, just take two bars of soap, we need soap only"

The bouncer did not want us to go but I guess the one who was giving orders was the boss.

"Hey, this lady has got money lets search her",

He said as he ran towards his group and left me and the cartman. I did not say anything to this guy since I suspected him to be part of the gang. I then reached for my handbag and gave him his money and we parted ways with him as I went to buy a bus ticket.

Our brothers are doing anything in this foreign land in order to survive. But how can they do that to one of their own I thought to myself. It means that these guys have been following me through my shopping. Thy must have realised that I had quite a lot of liduid cash on me so they decided to rob me of some of it. I had failed to exhaust the money on me and had resolved to keep it for another trip. The gang could not find an appropriate opportunity to attack me because I was always moving with the mob and at no time did I go to a lonely place, so they decided to wait until I get to a secluded place. Had they met me earlier then I would have not been able to buy anything.

I eventually boarded a bus that was bound for Bulawayo, after securing my luggage in the boot I got in the bus thinking of the meaning of every event that had happened during the trip. The trip was an eye opener to see exactly what is happening in the neighbouring countries where our mates are rushing to. I have heard that South Africa was worse than Botswana in terms of crime rate so I wondered what kind of a abyss it could be. I looked at my passport and thought of tearing off the South African Visa page in my passport. Even coming to hoard goods in this country was not safe, I realised that whatever I was thinking, I would not make it by going to another country.

A few kilometres before reaching the border the bus stopped for a recess. I wanted to ease myself so I got down to the rest room. I then went into a shop to buy myself a drink. There was a long queue in the shop as it was serving people from more than 3 buses parked at the stopover so I do not know how I must have delayed. When I got back, I found only one bus remaining and my blue bus had taken off. I was so busy in the shop that I did not hear the sound of the hooter that honked as the bus took off. I quickly ran to the remaining blue bus and then asked the conductor to offer me a ride to the border. I was now scared that we might not reach the border in time to get into my bus but the middle aged man whom I kept referring to Malume as he was affectionately called by his passangers reassured me that we will indeed meet at the border and I needed not to worry. All my luggage had gone with that bus. I was asked to pay 20 pula for the ride. I sat on the conductor seat in silence wondering what I would do if everything I had come to Botswana to bus gets lost. I was trying to gather my composure so that Malume does not see how worried I had become. I prayed to God to intervene in such a situation. By the time we reached the border my bus had already parked and the passengers had cleared from the Botswana side. I squeezed through the long queue so that I get cleared first and meet up with my fellow passengers. I realised that I was making a fuss for nothing. The process at the Zimbabwe side was so slow and hectic. Every piece of luggage had to be inspected that means that it had to be taken down from the carrier and boot and the bus would cross the weighbridge empty of luggage then we need to follow with the cleared luggage and pack again onto the bus. There ws an embargo on each commodity so people need to pay duty for any extras. The passengers were now busy exchanging goods so that they evade the tax. I was given some two boxes of baby cereal by one lady whom I gave my extra box of spaghetti. At the border while I was sorting my luggage I mistakenly stumbled upon the heavily pregnant woman wearing long white garments. The lady cried as if she was badly hurt. I was sure I did not do any harm to her I was about to complain to her for faking the pain when the employees at the customs office started to affront me for being careless and not considerate of the woman in such a condition. I felt so bad I kept saying sorry until she and her luggage were taken for priority clearing. The people at the customs kept referring to me as that lady who hurt a pregnant woman so much that I ended up making a joke out of it. After I got cleared, I went to our bus on the other side only to meet that woman eating a pie and a drink and laughing with her friends without any sign of heavy pregnancy. She looked at me and laughed and asked me to mind my own business. How she managed to fake pregnancy I was so amused. How can a woman play with my emotions like that for the sake of getting priority treatment at the border? She was probably smuggling something and had succeeded because her bag was hurriedly cleared. I just nodded my head and boarded the bus, it was none of my business after all.

The whole bus was full of groceries that were being bought from Botswana into Zimbabwe. My country was so impoverished that we could not afford our own basic commodities. Nevertheless, going to stay and survive on prostitution and shop lifting, robbery was not an option. After all, my health could not allow me to do that. I then decided to go back to the roots where I come from and strategize. It was time ask help of the ancestors.

We arrived in Bulawayo early in the morning and boarded a taxi to Bulawayo railway station. I was scared of getting robbed again so I teamed up with two other Harare bound travellers. We bought our tickets to Harare for the 8 pm train. After the robbery I had to settle for the cheap train which was now costing an equivalent of least than ten pula in the locally depreciated bearer cheques currency, I think it was around 50 billion dollars when the biggest note was 500 Billion dollars. If you look down the streets carefully you can stumble upon that money. The country currency had surpassed Germany in terms of losing value. They were busy printing the historic 100 trillion dollars note. I had made friends with two people a man and a woman whom I would leave in custody of my goods as I went to buy some food and shop around Bulawayo. We took turns to guard against theft of our goods as we took a walk around the second biggest city of Zimbabwe. I went to buy some fruits at the vegetable market with the remaining Bearer cheques I had after paying the bus fare. It was a hard time trying to buy anything using English language as a language of communication in Bulawayo. I realised that I needed to learn a bit of every language so that I can be able to communicate and buy freely in the countries bordering my own.

After more than 24-hour train ride I finally got back to Shona speaking Zimbabwe. Even though I had to endure a 1 hour delay between Norton and Harare due to power failure on the railway line I eventually arrived to find two of my friends waiting for me at the Harare international train station, I felt at home indeed. This journey gave me a different perspective about relocating to neighbouring countries. I decided to try and make it in my own country. With my condition I would not want to return home in a body bag.

Work

The next morning after I returned from Botswana when I woke up, looked at my phone I found a message from Pamela which said that I should come to her office, there was something she wanted to discuss with me. I found a reason to wake up go to the bathroom and get ready to get into town. Pamela was a friend who worked with the public service commission, we once met at a friend's party and I asked her to call if there arise an opportunity in the government. Apparently, she had found some job openings in the government ministries, she had kept her end of the promise all I needed to do was to reciprocate. I needed to choose where I want to go depending on my qualification. I decided to give it a shot, after all I did not need to go to a foreign land anymore after my experience in Botswana.

I started to process the whole set of papers so that I can get entry into working for the government. The process is so hectic and involves medical examination by a doctor, and clearance by the police.

"Do you have an illness that can affect your work", the doctor asked me during the medical examination.

I paused for a moment and then answered, 'No, I don't'.

I quickly decided to conceal my medical history, lest my condition led me to be denied acceptance in the civil service. I had thought very fast otherwise I would have replied in a manner that will jeopardise my employment with the biggest and generous employer in the country. The government was the least paying organisation in the country and as a result it was losing competent employees to neighbouring countries. The government had become a training ground for professionals who will later relocate to other countries. I decided to join the rest of the people in Zimbabwe and work for the government. The firm also offers good social services including, medical aid, pension and funeral service aid. It at least affords to take care of its employees in times of need. In addition, government employees have access to loans, and opportunities to further education and even foreign travel to other countries for education or exchange of skills. I focused on these advantages as I processed my papers for joining the firm.

My trip to deliver my papers to Ngungunyana building which is the headquarters of the Ministry of Agriculture presented me with great difficulty. I boarded a commuter omnibus which was bound for Borrowdale. Unfortunately, the vehicle had a tyre puncture at corner Josiah Tongogara and Borrowdale road. This is sensitive spot for a car to have a puncture. We got off before the presidential guards came. I had to finish the journey on foot. Ngungunyana building was less than a kilometre away. From nowhere this man who has gotten off from the same commuter started running towards me whilst panting like a racing horse.

"Hey, Sister wait I want to ask you something", I kept ignoring him knowing that it is not allowed to shout or make any suspicious movement around the State house. The Presidential residence is a heavily guarded premise in the country and the guards will deal with any suspicious activities accordingly.

The man kept running towards me. I decided to answer and warn about the protocol of the sacred place that we were in.

"Sorry Baba it is not allowed to talk or run in this place. This I the President's residence and you are supposed to behave your best. What did you want to ask?", I replied to him after he had continued running after me.

Before he could reply me a Palace guard just jumped from a tree right into our front like a Ninja. Holding a gun into his hand. I immediately knew that I was in big trouble.

"Hey, lovebirds what are you discussing here, are you arguing about how to throw your missiles on the Presidential residence. Who sent you and for how long have you been planning this? He asked us a lot of difficult and suggestive questions that we did not know which one to answer.

"I am sorry officer I am just explaining to this man about how to behave in this pathway', I eventually answered

"Yes, my son I was going to ask her where Hartman house Primary school is located", The other man replied.

I realised that this man will not take any of my explanations. He was bent on teaching us a lesson

We are sorry my brother please allow us to pass, we are sorry please.

I am not going to listen to any of you guys I have to take you up for attempting to Bomb the State house. Follow me he continued.

We continued to plead with him and he was giving us a cold shoulder. When we were about to reach the nearest gate.

I was contemplating on how I can negotiate my way out when suddenly another soldier came out of the gate and asked what was happening.

I explained my situation and so did the other man. Our statement did not contradict with each other so they decided to let us go. When we had taken two steps from where the one who had let us go then clarified his statement.

"There is no issue here you can just carry your daughter and go", he said. A sigh of relief struck me as I took my first step away from the soldiers.

"Hey, old man I said carry your daughter and go and I literally mean it'. The man ordered. We could not ask anything I just hoped onto his back and he held me the same way he would do to his little daughter. The punishment was better than getting inside the premise and be released when they feel like. I would miss an opportunity to get my employment papers that day and probably mean that I had to come back another day.

The old man had to carry me on his back until we reached an area which was out of sight of any palace guards. The poor man continued with his journey he did not say anything to me. I was walking behind him then I eventually turned to Ngungunyana Building at number 1 Borrowdale road. The encounter did not kill my morale, I had faced a lot of more bad situations than this one in the past month. The bad omen was still following me and I had to just ignore it and focus on my successful employment into the government.

I went to the department of Mechanisation Human resources department and handed over my papers to the receptionist who then returned to me about ten minutes letter with an employment contract that I field including the assumption of duty. From that minute onwards I was now officially an employee of the department of Mechanisation as Technician in the department of soil and water conservation. My place of work was going to be in the Provincial capital of Mashonaland central province.

Bindura

I was deployed to Mashonaland central province in the department of agricultural Mechanisation. My appointment brought a sigh of relief for me though it was going to be a hectic relocation to my province of origin. Bindura is the capital city of Mashonaland central. Located 88Km from the capital city of Harare it is a town whose economy is backed by mining and agriculture. The town houses the biggest nickel processing plant and the biggest nickel mine in Zimbabwe. It also has vast gold reserves which offers a source of living to most of the residents. It is indeed the development hub for the province. I was going to take part in the development of my own province. The economy was at its worst so I did not get any welcome from fellow members. Everyone was busy with running around to look for entrepreneurial ventures that are meant to bring food on the table.

I was sitting on an old desk in my new office when Masimba a fellow technician approached me. He greeted me with so much respect that I answered back calmly. I looked at the wedding ring in his finger and decided not to entertain him any further. I was trying to be careful with married men lest there will be a repeat of-the Maggie story. Contrary to what was on my mind the young man was just trying to welcome me. I eventually asked for the wifi password which he reluctantly gave me and we began talking. I realised that he was a different person so I even went on to ask him to help me with securing accommodation.

Petronella was the general hand and probably the safeguarding champion in the organisation. She took me into the storeroom and warned me about the repurcations of having intimate relationships with employees. I carefully listened as she narrated the related clauses on my contract.

'I heard you are not yet married and as the safeguarding champion of this office I decide to call you and warn you about these issues. Do not take an offence I do that to all new members of this office" she concluded as I left the room without giving any response.

I would go on my laptop and started googling about the Soccer World cup that was going to be done in South Africa the next month. I am a soccer fan who would not want to miss any detail about such tournaments. Masimba ended up joining me as we discussed the possible team line ups and made results prediction. I realised that I had a lot in common with Masimba and this made Petronella suspicious.

She could not stand our friendship that one day she shouted at me for loving soccer as if she was speaking to her daughter If it was not for Memory the Human resources officer I would have lost my cool.

"Hey Petronella if do not like soccer then let her be she is not a child everyone have their own hobbies and you must respect that" she told her .

"Hey Memory we come home from watching these things and then come here to hear cleopatra singing the same stories with her Masimba.

Masimba pulled me into the office and told me not to

mind her and continue with my day as usual. I realised that a spell of woman hating me always follow me. It took me a lot of time to befriend any other fellow woman at my workplace.

I grew so close to Masimba that I would visit his home on weekend and spend time with his wife and children. I ended up becoming a sister to him He would tell me about the different personalities we had in the office. I knew what to expect and how to behave when I meet each of the 22 employees of the Department. I eventually secured accommodation   in Chiwaridzo township. Apparently, Masimba's family was catholic so we would go for mass every Sunday at the Holy family catholic church in Bindura. Unlike in Budiriro where the whole neighbourhood was against me, Bindura was a complete opposite, people in the town

were not judgemental and they respected me. I began to grow up. I even bought myself some household furniture and a few quality clothes. Bindura was nearer my rural home so I could go home and get some blessings from my grandmother whenever I feel like. I would never miss the national holiday when I could visit my grandmother to keep her company lest she feels abandoned. My father's other children were staying with their mother and could just come for a few hours to see her and leave in their mother's car. Therefore, I needed to be there for her, after losing all her children. My grandmother had lost the zeal to live anymore.

Sangoma

One day I ultimately told her about my condition. I think that is when she came out of mourning, started to be there for me and tell me all the natural remedies that she had heard all the 82 years of her life.

"You should try everything because you never know what the pig ate to get that big body",

"Ok I will take whatever you gave me granny", I always said to her.

The Christmas that year was not like the usual Christmases that I have ever heard in my life. There was nothing to celebrate for this year. The rural home was empty without my uncle, and I was on a tough path that was difficult to walk in. I realised that all the earthly possessions were not sweet at all if one is in a difficult time. A lot had happened this year for me to hear the sounds of fireworks being popped by the children next door. Children that I will never have the privilege to bear. Grandma slaughtered a cockerel as usual but I did not enjoy its delicious taste because for one moment all the years problems had just hit back on my face. On the boxing day morning I woke up and went to the graveyard where my father and uncle were buried and I cried interminably.

I had to ask them how did they let such a predicament to befall me when they are there with the ancestors. They were supposed to talk to them and tell them to protect me.

They shouldn't have let it happen to me. "Why me? why me?", I cried while kneeling down beneath a tree at the graveyard.

"Cleo I need to take you to a Sangoma so that we establish the real cause of your problems", said grandma when we were having a cup of tea.

"Where is his coming from you know we are Christians", I replied but with a lot more questions running through my brain but with no apparent answer. I wondered if she had seen me on the graveyard in the morning, but it was still early for her to have followed me. I had stealthily left the room when she was still dead asleep. Furthermore, I had looked around and saw no one when I left the graveyard, I had cleaned myself up for anyone to think that I was crying. Maybe it is the old woman trying to use all the avenues to assist me.

"If you do not want then I will not force you i was only trying to help. There is this woman I know who lives in Kutsvaira village, she has helped many people who had your problems. Some things you just need to give it a try and maybe you can get healed", she continued as she tried to convince me.

'Its ok Gogo let's give it a shot", I replied in agreement. I did not want to disappoint the old woman who was just trying to help. After all, if I refuse and the situation get worse, grandma will not be able to forgive herself.

So after breakfast we hit the road and heard to Kutsvaira village to go and meet the lady traditional healer. Nothing fruitful was discussed during the 6Km journey to the Sangoma's house.

"This is my daughter whom I was talking to you about". said grandma after we made formal greetings to the middle-aged woman who doubled as a traditional healer and herbalist.

"Hey, she is a well-crafted woman, how can something like that happen to her it's so sad. Ok let us get to my shrine and hear what the spirits have to say about it, anyway who are we to decide what the spirits think", she replied as she led us to her shrine.

It was a small pole and dagga hut built at the easternmost corner of the 1 acre yard that was fenced by a live fence. We quietly followed as the lady led us to the huts.

"Remove your shoes, sit on the mat and wait for me", She instructed us, as we carefully followed blindly like we are taking army orders. The hut was divided by a traditional cloth popularly known as retso. I looked up and saw what looked like a python skin hanged above the traditional curtain. Right in the middle of the hut was hanging the skull of an animal, I wondered what kind of animal could have such a skull. I could see from the teeth that it was a carnivorous animal but I could not figure out which animal the skull belonged to. There was a corner full of clay pots and other things that I could not comprehend. As I was looking around the hut I saw the woman come back from behind the curtain and now she was covered in black and white cloth. Immediately, a young boy about ten years old came in and without greeting us he began to throw water on to the lady's body. I carefully observed as the woman started to make snakelike movements. The boy kept throwing droplets of water onto the woman who starred to make hissing sounds like a snake. She did all the snake manoeuvres until she sat on the mat. The mat was made of a skin of a leopard or maybe a cheetah. Upon sitting on the mat the lady roared like a lion. My heart jumped and the fear transferred to the body I jumped off and the small boy said.

"Do not be afraid woman, it is the ancestor who has arrived.', Grand ma held my hand tight. I think she too was hit by the fear but she tried to hold herself strong. My grandmother never exposed fear in front of people who depend on her. When I was a child one day, she bravely beat a mamba which was eating chicken eggs in her fowl run. I still remember the incident when my grandma hit the snake with a stick as I was freezing in fear. This is the incident that still gives me the courage to face my fears no matter what situation is presented in front of me.

"Who are these women in my shrine asked the Sangoma Lady in a hose voice. The voice sounded like an ailing old man who has had too much opaque beer.

I looked at the woman in amusement, how come the person who was speaking so normal moments ago just change completely to speak like an old man.

The young boy replied in a Vergie language that I could not understand?

"She is asking of your totem", the young boy said to us.

"Chihera", grandma replied.

The Lady continued mixing her herbs and threw down a number of stones which she uses to read into the life of her clients.

My totem is Chihera, the woman of Mhofu clan of Zimbabweans. The clan hold the eland so sacred that they do not eat it. The chihera woman are famous for being talkative, abusive and nagging. This time she was sitting and listening to the instruction of a spirit medium of the Moyo tribe. The spirit medium has the ability to be used by a spirit to convey messages that are helpful to solving life problems of people. At the time when he or she is possessed the customer can talk to the spirit and gets advice about how to solve the problems currently faced. The spirit can also tell you where the problem emanated from and advise you on how to deal with spiritual fights that you might not be aware of. The spirit can also diagnose an illness and prescribe traditional medicines to you. The medium will only be used as a tool for the spirit to execute its duties. This was the traditional form of hospital for the Zimbabweans which was used to take care of both physical and spiritual diagnostics of the human body. Long before hospitals come into place spirit mediums were used for spiritual, physical healings including physical wars. It is believed that spirit medium played an important role in the liberation struggle of Zimbabwe. They used to warn the soldier of the presence of an enemy and advise them on the route to take to avoid any confrontation with the Rhodesian armed forces.

"Who is Rwauya', the boy who was interpreting asked.

I never knew of anyone with such a name neither did grandma.

"We do not know of anyone by that asekuru", grandma replied.

"There must be someone in your lineage who had that name generations ago, he is probably forgotten now but if you ask elders of your family they definitely know about this story. The only surviving grandfather in my clan was Papa Joseph who was now blind and staying under the care of his married daughter in Masvingo since he is now a widower. He had developed dementia and cannot rightfully answer to any question. He does not remember my grandmother each time they meet and how on earth can we expect him to recall a story that happened over 3 generations ago. The man killed a servant way back and it is the spirit of this servant which is tormenting you, the servant is saying that he wants a wife from your tribe to give birth to a child who will replace his being on earth.

"Why is that happening to my children, she is not the only female in the family", grandma asked her voice shivering with so much agony.

"The spirit of the servant has chosen her and she cannot have a child for any other man that is why I see that her womb is closed. The doctors will diagnose it as cancer but it is the spirit of that person".

"Oh my God can someone listen to this", I asked myself silently as the interpreter continued with the explanations.

"So, what can we do to save my child', replied grandma with tears almost flowing down her left eye. This explanation will definitely increase her already compromised blood pressure. The woman had always adored my achievements. She was a proud grandmother who would do anything to see her grandchild happy. Now, it seems impossible henceforth. The old lady was feeling for me even though I was not moved by any of the statements. I saw them as people who were acting out and expecting us to believe.

"What you need to do is to go to the river tomorrow morning and wash your body from the water from a spring commanding the spirit to leave her. You will need a white hen, 4 eggs and a litre of cooking oil, 2 new razor blades and coarse salt", instructed the interpreter.

"Do you have any questions' she continued

"Who exactly was the slain servant where was he from and how can we get to appease his spirit that is tormenting my daughter", asked grandmother.

"You are all women come with a man of the family next time to get answers to that", the sangoma replied.

These are the only words that I managed to comprehend from her because of her tone and deep language I definitely needed an interpreter to help. She was talking in a very strong language and strange tone for any layman to understand. She instructed that in the meantime while we wait for male members of the family, we would need to undertake a cleansing ceremony to drive away this spirit from me and leave it in water so that it   stops bothering me. Unless another member of the family goes and try calling up evil spirits from the river then the spirit will be wondering in water and not able to attack anyone.

'What else do we need for the cleansing ritual', I asked because I did not want to get any surprises the next day.

'You might need clothes to change into after the cleansing ritual" replied the little boy.

"I am going now; the lady roared like a lion and finally came back to herself. She began speaking with a normal voice and talking in the shona language . I was so surprised to see how the spirit medium operates. It was such an adventurous first encounter with a Sangoma. All my life I had never gone to witness the spirit medium in operation.

She asked the boy what the spirit had said. Surprisingly she too does not have to hear herself talking like that and get to comprehend what the spirit had said. She had to rely on the ten year old. The boy was so intelligent and so pure to carry out the job. The spirit would want the shrine to be worked by small children who have not known a woman their life and not corrupted adulterous grown man. The interpreter would rather be a very old man or woman who are no longer having sex and not the sexually active individuals.

The boy narrated to her everything including other things that we did not understand.

"Are you going to do what the spirit commanded', I nodded in agreement.

"You are free to consult other spirit mediums and then compare the findings and let's hope it won't be too late for the young woman".

Nobody uttered a word as we left the shrine and embarked on our 6Km journey back home. I was now very hungry I only stopped to pick some wild berries called Mazhanje in the forest to quench my hunger. The Wild berries were now getting finished in the forest I was lucky to come across a tree that had many ripe, fallen and sweet ones from the ground. It was probably one of the few trees remaining in the forest and no one had passed through it on the day that is why a gathered so many. Grandma just ate a few she was not fond of the fruits and even at home she used to gather them a keep them for sale rather than for own consumption. As we sat, we saw a springbok pass by. The springbok is a sacred animal of the land of Msana. Coming across a springbok is a sign that the Gods of the land are with you. If you are doing anything against the rules of the land you will see one that will be having 3 legs and you get confused and fail to find your way back. Many have gotten lost in the forest and were found about 3 days later after crossing the Msana boundary into neighbouring Domboshava. Once found the land spirit medium will have to do a cleansing ceremony for the person to gain their sanity back. The Msana land is a rich sacred sanctuary that is a remake of the great Zimbabwe. It is believed that another group of the Rozvi people had settled in the land where they build structure similar to the great Zimbabwe which is held sacred to this day.

I tried to recall any stories that I was told by my uncle Mike but not any day did I hear him mention about an ancestor killing a servant. Could it be that it happened more than 5 generation ago? If it indeed happened then why has this evil spirit chose to torment me. I am not the only descendant of my clan. I am probably the unlucky one but why, I asked myself many questions with no one to answer.

I resolved to go ahead with the cleansing ritual for the sake of my grandma. If I was alone then I could have ignored it. The old lady had volunteered to go with me that far and face the consequence all for my sake I just had to comply.

Cleansing

We woke up as early as 4 am for the journey to the hot spring. We were going to meet the Sangoma and her assistant there. All the fear of the dark and early morning goblins vanished. My grandmother was there with me to take me there. I was following behind my grandma when she suddenly stopped. The washing area was just about 200metres away and the sun was beginning to come out. She took out her hand to stop me. I looked at the road to see what had made her to suddenly stop. I looked up and I saw a 1.5metre long python crossing the path. The creature was moving stealthily since it was in its own home. It was probably tired after a night's hunt. It was not in a hurry to cross the road so it was taking its time. We all stood still without talking to each other. I believe that people can communicate even in silence. My grand ma and I must have discussed what to do as we all moved back silently and took an alternative road towards the mountain where the spring was located.

Nobody uttered a word until we got to where the Sangoma and her assistant were seating.

"I saw that the spirits were following you do not despair a python is a good spirit that I work with and it was showing you that you are in the right path. I remembered the python skin that I had seen in her shrine and realised that this woman was also using the spirits of a python to do her magic and indeed we needed not worry as the spirit was possessing the python that we saw on our way to the spring.

She quickly dressed up and instructed me to follow her. We kept climbing up to the main spring that supplies water to the Nyazvidzi river. The place is very sacred and I have heard many stories about people disappearing or going mad after entering this sacred place. There I was following some grown woman in that sanctuary. After a few minutes we had reached a rock which was presumably her second spring. She immediately knelt down and began enchanting to the ancestors telling them that she had brought their child who mean no harm but will seek permission to be cleansed and guided by the sacred waters. Meanwhile I was there kneeling down like a newly wedded wife and having no idea of the next step. I was asked to lead the way to the water and step into the water just under the running waterfall. I hesitated as I set my first foot into the cold water. Nevertheless, I carefully stepped into the water to end up just under the waterfall. The spring water was very cold but I bravely stood beneath it. The woman then followed me with a bag of herbs. She took an egg and break it into my forehead. I had permed hair but I had to forget all that and allow myself to go through the cleansing process. She took another egg, cooking oil and a number of herbs including coarse salt and mixed it in a wooden plate and smeared everything on my forehead and the stomach just below the navel. She was saying some words in a language that I could not understand.

She then dived into the pool and disappeared for a while. I waited enraged with a feeling of fright and enthusiasm mixed in one. For a moment I asked myself what I will say to grandma and her assistant if she does not make it back. The two were left about 50 meters away and were not aware of what was happening under the waterfall. I got relieved when she rolled out of the water holding two shells and sand, these items were taken from the deepest part of the waterfall. She made me hold it tight in my hand as she continued splashing me with the water coming from the spring.

"Did you bring clothes to change", she asked after she was convinced with the wash.

'Yes, in my bag I left it with granny 'I replied.

'You can go and change into them', she instructed me as she moved out of the water.

I got out of the water and straight to my grand ma. I was shivering all the way when I took the bag which had my clothes, hid behind a bush and changed into fresh clothes. The exercise was so cruel to my body. The herbs had a foul smell and I was not allowed to comment it was as if I was an object that was being cleaned. I went back to the spring-side shrine and I found the Sangoma now seated and beside her was a fire. Her assistant had made a fire all this time that I was being washed in the water. She then instructed me to kneel down near the fire with my eyes facing the glowing fire. She sprinkled some herbs onto the glowing fire and covered me with traditional cloth. She did not mind my sneezing and coughing I guess that is what she was trying to induce by the procedure. After 2 or so minutes she removed the cloth and gave me mutton fat to smear onto my face. The fat from mutton is popular for driving away evil spirits. She then took a razor blade and pierced a little on my back and smeared some herb mixture onto me. She then took another blade and made an incision into the skin beneath my navel and smeared the same herbs.

"Gogo we have finished the first part of helping your daughter and all you need to do now is go back home. From here to you place do not look back or talk to anyone along the way. Take this lamb fat and mix it with your lotion and do not let any other person use your lotion. Also take these roots when you get home crash it and add two litres of water. Let it settle overnight and drink the medicine for 3 days. Come back after 3 days and tell me your dreams and it is your dreams that determines the next steps. Do you have any questions?" She finished with her instructions.

For sure I needed a book or recorder to get all those instructions. I had to bath while facing east after mixing a certain herb for the next three days at the same time and saying out certain words which I was instructed. I had to fetch firewood from a Muhacha tree which I had to pick from a tree and not gather fallen twigs, I had to use that firewood to boil Water mixed with another set of herbs and steam with that water every night for three days after bathing and before going to bed. I had also had to drink a raw egg mixed with milk and oil and was expected not to vomit. Some of the instructions I can no longer remember. I was not supposed to talk to anyone until l get home and sprinkle the ashes from the shrine fire. Honestly how can I avoid people in my own neighbourhood and I was not allowed to turn back to the shrine until I reach home how difficult it is to keep your head up not look back for 6km. It looked as an easy task but it was not. I also had to write down my dreams for the three days that I will be taking the said concussions. that I had to remember my dreams for 3 nights was a mammoth task.

"You need to ask now Cleo lest you forget, did you understand anything".

"Yes Gogo, I got everything'.

We left the shrine and headed back home. We needed not look back so we did not look back even if we hear anything from behind us. Grandma was leading the way using a very unpopular road to avoid meeting people.

We eventually got home after a long struggle.

I managed to do what the Sangoma had told me to do. On the third night I had a dream in which I was being pursued by wild animals that looked like hyenas in a mountain. I was running so hard and going uphill. I could not breathe properly and suddenly I saw a cliff at the end. I was now between the animals and a cliff. I decided to jump into the cliff. The dream felt real as I fell into a gorge. I fell into a pool of very cold water. I sank so deep that I failed to breathe as I struggled to get up, I woke up kicking all the blankets and screaming like someone coming from a deep dive. My grandma was sleeping next to me. The woman heard me; I must have been making movements during my sleep but she had decided not to wake me up.

"Are you alright Cleo", she asked me as I opened my eyes. My body was full of goose bumps like a dressed chicken.

I woke up and looked at the watch. The time was almost 3 am so I went out to ease myself. The next morning, I told my grandmother about my dream. It is a taboo in the Shona culture to tell someone about your dream before sunrise the next morning.

When we went back to the sangoma and told her about my dream. She interpreted it as a sign of victory to my battle. I had to go back drink some herbs and expect full recovery after 3 months. My grandmother was happy about the development and hoped for the best for me.

Chinembiri

Even though my grandmother was convinced about the Sangoma I insisted on seeking a second opinion. I asked aunty Agness's Mother Manyoni and she directed me to a sangoma who lived in Chiweshe where she hailed from. Apparently the sangoma was in the area helping a certain family and it was up to us to approach him before he returns to his place. I told my grandmother and we took off to Jonasi village where he was helping solve problems of the Simboti family. When we arrived at the homestead there were a number of people from different families who also wanted to sought the help of Chinembiri the great Sangoma. There was a queue so we joined the, and wait for out turn to see this spiritual man. Within half an hour 3 families had been assisted. He came out and look at the queue and sprinkled some water on the one lady who was next in line. I was surprised when I saw the daughter about 15 years old changing mood and began to look angry as if she wanted to beat someone. Her mother asked her if there is any problem and she began to be violent and took a boulder and wanted to attack her mother for asking. Chinembir came back and smiled then sprinkled some water on the girl who then passed out. They carried her into the hut and then minutes later her father ran to his home to bring the pillow which he was using. When he arrived with the pillow the Sangoma came out with the entire family and he asked the man to put the pillow on the ground as he started to sprinkle water on it while making some incarnations which we could not understand. He took a knife and cut through the pillow and grabbed an object which he told everyone that it is a goblin. It was a mysterious item that someone was using to bewitch the daughter. He then asked the brother of the man who was the owner of the pillow to come and hold this thing if he claims that he is clean. The guy came and when he was about to hold the goblin he fell on his back like a tree. Everyone thought he was dead. The sangoma went back inside with the family members, maybe he was explaining to them the meaning of the incident. The man continued to lie on the ground and everyone was scared that he might be dead struck by a goblin in our very eyes. They came back and the Sangoma resuscitated him. He was still in confusion and the sangoma jokingly gave him the Goblin again and he was extending his hands when the brother shouted

"Musabate Simboti" meaning do not hold the thing simboti. The brother still had a portion of love for his sibling regardless of allegations of witchcraft that was directed towards his daughter. It was a great display of sibling love that I was witnessing that day. They took the goblin away and instructed the man never to do any witchcraft lest he dies because he had cast a reversal spell on any family member who would want to harm anyone.

Chinembiri was quite a spectacular Sangoma you would spend the whole day watching as he exposed wizards and witches in the neighbourhood. Before we knew, it was our turn to court him. His makeshift shrine was not very scary since he was just hanging a red cloth in the abandoned kitchen that once belonged to the Simboti Grandparents and since their death no one was keen to use the kitchen since all the children had built their own.

"what can we do for you Grandma,"asked Chinembiri

"I am here with my grandchild,'" answered Grandma.

"Its ok I can see that she was diagnosed with an uncurable illness and you are so worried" He started

Chinembiri had managed to read into my problem without asking anything. I began to slowly believe in traditional healing. He went on teling us about our recent cleansing. He told me the exact plan of the house which I live in Bindura as well as our house in the village. He agreed to an evil spell of a slain person following me everywhere I go and this is being perpetrated by a female relative who is jelous about my achievements.

"Who is this woman"asked grandmother eventually.

"I will not tell you but I will give you some herbs so that you see her for your self. The woman is aware of what you have done and have gone to Chipinge to see a great wizard of the waters called Ndunge if you know him. She will reverse the spell and all your efforts will be in vain"explained the Sangoma

"So, what can we do to stop this catastrophe", asked grandma with tears almost flowing down her tiny cheeks.

"Ok Young lady go back home and take the bucket of mealie meal which you are using and the ashes that you threw away today".

I stood up and left the room without asking any further questions. I came back with the requested items. I found grandma seated and chatting with a group of ladies about what had just happened. The family that had came after us had a elderly man who was using juju to sleep with most ladies in the Jonasi village. The old man came back with his charm which was a male private part decorated with some beads. The man had confessed to using it on most people including his brothers wives, his daughters in laws, and even his daughters. He was the reason why most of the daughters of the family are unwed or return to their husband's houses.

I put my bucket of mealie meal down and the Sangoma sprinkled some water onto the ashes and then smeared the mixture onto his hands. He then opened the bucket and brought out something that looked like a purse. When we looked closer the thing looked like a tiny weaving bucket which was decorated with beads.

"This is the mode of communication that is used to monitor your every move. The woman is always ahead of you and knows your plans. Confiscating this thing made her blind so that you can plan your move without her knowledge. Inthree days she will come and you will see her. What you need to do is to take this water and thereherbs then put into your bedroom. You will not sleep in your bedroom but rather sleep in the kitchen for the next three days you will see the woman who is causing you problem. When you see her she will be powerless and the healing that the other Sangoma gave you woll work.

We did exactly as told and on the third night just before midnight I woke up to a sound of a falling object. I opened my eyes and saw Auntie Barbra sitting in the ashtray. To my surprise aunt Barbra was a very huge woman how come she could fit in an ash tray.

Apparently Aunt Barbra was my father's niece. She was a successful woman who carried herself as a devoted member of the ZAOGA apostolic faith church. The woman would despise you for mingling with drunkards and would not talk to you if she sees you drinking beer. I would not have thought that she would do that. I could not believe my eyes when I woke up Grandma who was sleeping next to me.

"Grandma look there is Aunt Barbara in the ash tray. My grandmother could not see anything but she managed to sprinkle salt into the ash tray and started to pray so strongly. I was also praying at the same time I was in much confusion. If this is indeed the truth then we should not judge a book by its cover. The lady was stuck in the ash tray until around 4 in the morning. I could not get a wink of sleep.

We went back to Chunembiri to get hints of the way forward. He told me not to worry and expect full healing by the prescribed time by the first Sangoma. I went back to work in the new year. The new year brought with it a high hope for complete recovery and getting my life back on track again. After 3 months I went for another diagnosis to see if the traditional medicine had worked. To my surprise the disease was just dormant I had to keep doing what I was doing to avoid development of the disease. Much to my amusement because I had thought that I would get zero detection of the disease in my body after going through all the traditional processes.

Chapter 11 Ruka.

I had to go and spend the Easter holiday with my grandmother, so I took the bus from Bindura to Nyava. It was the shortest route to my rural home but it involved finishing the last 10Km on foot. I was carrying a bagful of goods that I had brought for my grandma. The luggage was so heavy I had to stop at every 1Km peg to rest and then continue until I reach my destination. When I had walked for about 3Km and about to make a stop I saw a man dressed in a khaki short, a Liverpool jersey and a pair sandals walk towards me. He had just come out of the side road and was going in the same direction as me.

"Good afternoon", I greeted him respectfully as I put down my sack and ready to take the third rest.

"Hey Cleo is that you, it has been a long time and you have grown so big how are you" he replied with mush jubilation

The man had identified me and knows my name it was going to be rude if I had asked him who he was.

"Yes, its me how are you too", I smiled back while forcing a smile on to my face.

The guy must have seen that I had not recognised him even if I was trying to hide it.

"Its me Ruka have you forgotten; I am the one who used to stay at the Chimbama homestead when you were still kids. We used to tease you when you were going to school all those years ago. Now I am staying in your village. So where are you staying now. The man said as he stopped on the same shed that I was taking a rest.

I had remembered him. He used to herd cattle for the Chimbamas when I was in high school. He doubled the job with looking after the homestead of the Harare based family. Ruka had lived to be part of the village to the extent that Mr Mandebvu the village head gave him his own piece of land when he married his niece. Ruka had become a part of the village that he was regarded as one even if he was from unknown origins. The rumours had it that he was raised by his grandmother after his mother died while giving birth to him. Ruka could not go to school beyond primary school because he did not have a birth certificate. Nobody knew his father since his mother died before telling anyone the name of the man who had gotten her pregnant. His uncles could not assist in getting him a birth certificate. The Chimbamas took him as cattle herder ever since and tasked him to take care of their house. When his grandmother died, he moved to stay at the Chimbama homestead until he got married to Mr Mandebvu's niece Carol. Now the Chimbamas are settled permanently in the country and are no longer fond of city life, their children are all grown up and have moved to the United Kingdom for better life.

I told him where I was coming from and tried to make it short so that he can continue with his journey and leave me to continue with my rest.

'oh ok I see you have been doing well but as you were talking the holy spirit showed me that you have something troubling you", he said as he sat on a stone just a few meters from where I was standing. The move showed me that Ruka was not planning to go but was eager to tell me a lot of things. Could I be that this man is sent to help me? I wondered how the boy we used to kick the soccer ball with can now talk to the holy spirit. I sat down as well and listened to what he had to say.

Ruka told me everything about me from the place I was born, my parents, what I had gone through in my life up to now. Most of the stories I had not shared with anyone but this holy spirit had shown him. I was surprised with his kind of diagnosis. He even told me about my condition, how I had gone to seek the help of traditional healers and how I had gotten disappointed by the results of the doctors recently. The guy did it like he was holding a mirror and following my every move. I believed that he had some kind of spirit that uses him. That same spirit should be used to bring solutions to my problems. Ruka belonged to the Nguwo tsvuku" Red garment church" where he had grown to be a renowned spiritual healer in the entire Mashonaland Central Province.

However, according to him, my problems were being caused by a woman close to me. I wondered because the woman who was closest to me was my grandmother. It is not possible for the person who wants to see me happy to be the cause of my problem.

"No, its not your grandmother, it is someone who shares the same totem as you that is your sister, cousin or Aunt," , he must have read my mind when he said this statement. He was not going to tell me which one of the two to avoid the possibility of confrontation but he probably did not see that I was aware of who it was from the Chinembiri escapades the previous holiday.

After a while of probing and not getting answers I then asked him for a way forward, Ruka said that he will visit my place and talk it over in the presence of my grandmother.

I stood up and carried my luggage and started to move. Ruka then offered to carry my luggage for me until he gets tired. He would reach his house first before me so he carried it from my had to his and began walking towards our village. He was moving so fast that I who was carrying a handbag had to sometimes run after him to keep up with his speed. All the way I had been trying to persuade him to tell me the name of the person who has cast an evil spell on me. What did she want from me, how will she benefit from it. Ruka kept insisting that he will explain everything in front of my grandmother. He must have been afraid to tell me the name in order to avoid any possible family feuds.

About 600meters from my house Ruka bade me farewell as he turned into a strip road to his home. I took my luggage and finished the remaining 600metres to get home to my unsuspecting grandmother.

I could see my grandma's happiness as I stepped into the compound. As usual she was sitting on the stoop basking in the late afternoon sunshine.

"Titambire" , she exclaimed as she tried to stand up to greet me", I immediately put my luggage down to properly greet my old woman.

"Hey I am so tired I have walked all the way from Nyava", I said as I sat down on the stoop next to her.

"I had forgotten the distance I almost fainted and was resting every kilometre", I continued.

I had gone to Nyava high school an could walk the 10km journey to and for everyday throughout my secondary school life. This time I was struggling because I had grown so much fat. As I rested, I told my grandmother about my journey and the story of Ruka, how he told me about my life and told me about the source of my problems. My grandmother was carefully listening this whole time and waiting for me to finish. My grandmother was a great listener who never interrupts anyone until they finish. She had become the sweet aunt to her brothers children to whom she always provided a listening ear. She was not judgemental and was free to give her opinion and not force a person to adopt her opinion. One after the other the nieces and nephews will come for various advises ranging from marital, sibling rivalry, business and personal development.

"Did you believe him", she finally asked after I had made my final statement.

"No, but he told me things that are true about me he is probably being used by a good spirit, you will see him he will come here tomorrow and you can ask him other questions",I replied.

The whole night I did not get a wink of sleep wondering what the meaning of my encounter was. Could it be that the holy spirit was working through Ruka. I had met spiritual healing each time I visited the village. The last time it was my grandmother and sangoma. And this time I bumped into the man of cloth who was willing to help, we were in the holy week and maybe it was the God's reply. It was probably the longest night that I had endured all my life. Thoughts are major cause of insomnia more than any other condition. I had become a victim of spiritual healing each time I visited my village. Sourcing spiritual help was never a common procedure in my family. Growing up I had seen my grandmother never visit a spiritual man of any sort for any personal problem. It was only one time when her brother Nick lost a child and the wife was accusing aunt Teererai for using black magic to kill her baby. Aunt Teererai cried like a toddler in my very eyes after most of the aunties and grand aunts failed to listen to her plea.

"How could I have killed a baby. I know I am barren but I never wish for a child to die', she exclaimed.

The 3 months old baby had caught illness just after Auntie Teererai and her husband visited the baby and left some clothes as a push present for the child. They accused Teererai of using juju on the clothes to kill the child. From that incident onwards aunt Teererai is never to give presents to new-borns or even to visit juveniles. She just congratulates from where ever she is. In this era of social media communications, she just congratulates over the phone. She cannot bear to go through the same predicament.

The next morning Ruka came to our home and found us all waiting for him. He was now carrying a bagful of his red garment which he puts on while conducting his spiritual healings.

"Gogo I had watched this girl grow up and would want to see her raise her own children. She is quite a woman any man would love to have as a wife', He said as he dressed himself up in preparation for his spiritual healing. He then started singing his hallelujah song which we just had to sing along as he sprinkled water on me and my grandma. The man started to make some roaring sound like that of a lion. I looked up to see what he was doing. He instructed me to look to the east, he picked up 3 stones and told me to throw them while praying and telling the lord what I want,. I had to say it aloud and specific.

"Dear lord I want you to remove the cancer that is eating my womb and allow me to get married and have children'", I shouted while I threw those stones away in an eastward direction.

Grandma please give me 3 eggs and a wooden plate.

Grandma just got up to her fowl run and came back with 3 eggs. He put the eggs in a wooden plate and made a loud prayer that was concluded with some tongues that I could not comprehend.

He gave me the eggs one by one and told me to throw them back just above my head.

"Cleo be serious", shouted my grandmother when I was about to throw my last.

I angrily threw them back and when I turned to look back all the eggs had not broken. I wondered how eggs that can break by merely rubbing against each other can fail to break after being thrown onto a hard surface.

"Now you see what I have been telling you. The spirit following you is very strong I need a white spotless chicken to take it out and allow you to be cleansed. I was lucky that Grandma had some broilers that she was selling and she took one remaining one and gave it to him. Ruka held the chicken an began his prayers. He asked us to join him.

"You should pray so hard for the evil spirits to leave you.

I began my very powerful silent prayer. I needed to get healed an it is me who had brought this man to my house without asking for my grandmother consent. The healing was supposed to be worth it because it had taken a lot from me.

Ruka took the fowl and made it step on my forehead, my chest and my lower abdomen. He then commanded it to take all the evil that was on me. Making circular movements around my head he put the fowl onto the ground and the animal breathed its last. He then gave me the eggs to throw again and this time all the eggs broke like there are supposed to. He then instructed me to take my lotion and a bottle of water. He prayed for them and told me to use them until finished.

When the procedure was completed I went into the kitchen to make a cup of tea for our visitor whilst I left him talking to my grandma. After breakfast Ruka took off to his house he had finished his task.

Immediately after he left I made preparation to go for the good Friday mass. The stations of the cross procession was going to start soon near our home. I never would want to miss this special day in the Christian calendar. I joined the rest of the congregation in re-living the final moments of Jesus Christ. I wept on all the 13 Stations of the cross. The whole procession I was thinking about my own situation. I felt God's presence in me and I could go straight to heaven on that day. I spent the entire holiday enjoying my purity and sinless life I believed all my sins were forgiven on that day.

Stroke

I had made friends with almost all the people that I was working with to the extent that it felt like family more than colleague. And when the news of the sickness of Jakarasi was told to the office everyone was devastated. The guy had been sick for some time and no one ever knew that it would get this worse. He was taken to Bindura hospital where he was battling for survival. The doctor had diagnosed him of multiple organ failure and he needed to immediately go on dialysis in Harare. All the paper work were being processed when suddenly the office land line rang. It was rare for the office line to ring because it was always engaged. Fortunately, on this day everbody was busy with gathering information that was required by the Minister as soon as yesterday for them to be on the phone. Mai Charamba the receptionist answered it and we could just hear her making a loud scream.

Mr Jakarasi had passed away. A cloud of sorrow engulfed the office as people broke down to tears. Mr Jakarasi was a middle-aged artisan who knew well how to do his job. He never quarrelled with anyone and was ever smiling The man loved his beer, he is one man who could hope from clear beer, to opaque beer, to whiskies and wines without any problem. He was not a smoker but a heavy drinker who would shiver if he did not have any alcohol in his body. It is probably, the alcohol dependency that had led to his kidneys to fail , leading to multiple organ failure that eventually took his life. The organisation then organised for staff members to support his family throughout this difficult time. The man was to be buried in Chiweshe where he hailed from.

My tears flew uncontrollably as i saw his rural home that he was building. Apparently, Mr Jakarasi had two wives all independent women who could take care of themselves his mother was alive and bearing the pain of losing a child. I was devastated by the sight of his eldest daughter crying over the loss of her father. I could recall myself in the same situation all those years ago. Your father is always your hero regardless of what everyone says or thinks about them. The first love, the protector and the person who offers you shed and protection from earthly harm. I had lost all my fathers and I could feel for the young girl. She had to be taken from school to bid farewell to the lifeless body of her father. As they lowered the coffin, I began to feel powerless in the right side. Both the arm and legs felt detached from me one could even put a red-hot stove on my right hand and I could not feel anything. This was my first experience of a stroke.

I asked Chiedza who was standing next to me to hold me tight so that I do not fall down. Chiedza complied and slowly escorted me to the nearest vehicle. I asked for cold water, when I was given the water some power was beginning to come back. Everyone who saw this must have thought that I was so much in pain over my friend's death.

I was surprised also about the development. I was able to walk again as if nothing had happened to me but internally, I was in shock. Me having a stroke how could it wait to happen at a friend burial site. Everyone looked at me with questions in their eyes. Questions that I had no answers to. The next morning I went to my doctor who told me that it was a form of mild stroke due to high blood pressure. I was immediately put on aspirin based high blood pressure treatment. I had developed another problem to add to what I already have. I was born in a family who had a history of high blood pressure although my father and uncle Mike were never diagnosed of any such condition. My grandmother was a hypertension patient who was popping nifedipine everyday of her life. My mother was also depending on some hypertension lifetime pills. It was something that I was expecting but for it to come when I am having to deal with another life-threatening situation was something I never expected. Now life had to bring me every predicament that is lying in my path so that even if I die early, I would have had a taste of everything.

Chapter 12 Mtemwa.

The stroke is one problem that I decided to keep to myself. I never got to tell my grandmother lest she have a stroke too. I kept this problem to myself. I then decided to use my catholic belief to the best of my advantage. I had heard of Mtemwa leprosy centre where my fellow catholics and even non-catholics would go for spiritual and physical healing. A lot of people who visited the shrine bear testimonies of total healing from various uncurable ailments such as cancer, barenness and even leprosy.

I went there accompanied by my friend Maria who is also Masimba's wife. Maria believed that if you pray and go to the top of the mountain where Saint John Bradburne used to drink water from all your problems will be solved. There were many testaments of people from as far as

South Africa and United Kingdom who had visited Mtemwa and got themselves healed from numerous diseases and conditions. John Bradburne is a catholic martyr who worked in Mtoko in the 1970s. He went there on a pilgrimage and decided to take care of lepers who lived at an isolated place near Mtemwa hill in Mtoko. To reduce the spread of leprosy people of Mtoko used to isolate lepers and abandoned them at an isolated place just beneath the Mtemwa hill where they would eventually die. Well-wishers would occasionally bring them food. John decided to work for the lepers full time. He sourced funds to build the Mtemwa leprosy centre and also sourced medicine for their healing. He was a spiritual healer who would pray for a person and the person would get healed. He then became very popular and because it was the era of the armed struggle he was mistaken for a sell out and slain. He had performed a lot of miracles that even his funeral proceedings was characterised by several miracles. Three drops of blood dripped from his coffin to symbolise the holy trinity. People even go to his grave to take the soil from his grave as they believe it has some healing power. Ever since his death people have gone to Mtemwa to see remaining lepers who would narrate the good work of Bradburne. People would climb the Mtemwa hill to get to the topmost part where John used to go and pray everyday. On the mountain top there is a well of water which people deem anointed which they fetch to cleanse themselves of various ailments. A lot of people have testified complete healing after visiting the Mtemwa shrine. Upon hearing many stories of healing i decided to embark on a journey to the east.

We arrived at Mtemwa at about sunset and we got to meet

the lepers who narrated to us the story of John Bradburne first hand. We sat in the hut with others and also watched a movie on the biography of John Bradburne. We then embarked on the journey up the mountain we were led by one tout from the centre. We were quite a number of people of all ages who had come from various corners of Zimbabwe who had their problems that they needed to pray about. No one wanted to talk to anyone but we all concentrated on saying the station of the cross at every designated station until we reach the mountain top. On the mountain top everyone was given time to pray their own prayers. I prayed like I never prayed before because I wanted my problem to disappear. I wanted to bear testimony of total healing from the centre. I sang, prayed while standing, prayed while kneeling down, until I was satisfied that I have prayed enough. We sat at the mountain top singing holy songs waiting for the spectacular sunrise from the mountain top. The sunrise from the mountain top is very spectacular and some would mistake it for a miracle. After sunrise we began to go down the mountain and embarked own our journey back to the capital.

We were given a lift by a fellow catholic couple whom we have met at the shrine. The commuter omnibus we were travelling with was full of people who had just been blessed by the visit to the shrine. One woman even claimed to have seen a vision of Virgin Mary and a child and she interpreted it as a total healing to her barenness. I kept communicating to the woman who got pregnant just a month after the visit and is now a proud mother of twins a boy and a girl. Anot her man claimed to have see a man dressed like john bradburne coming towards the well and blessing the water while we were praying. It seemed that half of the people abode the bus had some visions which they experienced. I was not to be discouraged I thought that maybe next time I will experience a vision of my own.

Henry

When I visited my grandmother for the heroes holiday I had found myself a new boyfriend. I was glowing again ad I was for a bit of time slowly forgetting about my problems. I had met Henry at a work-related workshop at the Village Lodge in Gweru. Henry was an engineer working for the Ministry of water. Ours was love at first sight. We connected quickly started chatting over social media networks. He was probably following my social media life because he was the first to comment on everything that I posted. I decided to give the poor guy a chance after all he was still not married maybe we could strike some agreement and start a life together. Hoping that my cancer does not spread to early. The guy was so into me that I was surprised. He practically behaved like my husband. He could come to my house and be the man of the house. I had learnt to play the woman of the house when I visited him in his two roomed flat that he rented in Avondale.

"Have you told him about your condition", asked grandma when we were shelling the remaining maize. Grandma was the best farmer in the neighbourhood. She would achieve a bumper harvest because of her crop husbandry skills that she had learnt from the Extension officers who practised long before the country attained its independence. Grading of maize was one task she never missed when she was processing maize. The healthy and big cobs she would hand shell them first and treat the maize for future personal use. The extra of the good maize will be sold to other people in January when some people's grain reserves would have dwindled. These small and pest infected maize that we were shelling could be used for stock feed. It will be sold to those farmers for feeding their livestock.

"No, grandma, I do not know how and what to say to the innocent man", I replied

Grandma had the sentiments that I should tell the person who loved me everything. I should not hide anything to him lest I get him disappointed. Man are not emotionally strong and it is always good not to play with their emotions.

"Its already too late grandma, he is not going to forgive me. I do not want to hurt his feelings", I continued.

My grandmother took almost an hour explaining to me the consequences of my actions. My grandmother believed that you should not hide information from your partner. She believed that one should accept you the way you are should not be taken by surprise. She then continued and lectured me on the values of marriage that she always exhibited during her own marriage. How she managed to forgive her husband when he cheated on her while trying to look for more children. It looked like she was preparing me for marriage.

The thought of marriage was never on my mind how could I even think of that with my condition. The only problem was Henry who was growing too close to me. I actually needed to find ways of driving him away lest he become too attached to me. It will be difficult to leave me if he gets so much into me. I stopped for once and thought that I was being unfair to Henry however it was not going to be easy to tell him this problem. Actually, I did have many more problems for him to handle. He knew that I was a BP patient when he visited me and saw the BP tablets that I had kept with me.

When I got back to work I decided to drop the bombshell to him. The poor man froze for a moment before he could say anything. He was probably stuck between the snake and the deep waters. I could see that he was confused. On that day he failed to even give me a goodnight kiss. At least I had told him and taken off the stress from me. The ball was in his court and whatever decision he make I would take it. The next morning, he left early in the morning without saying anything concerning my health. We kept communicating over social media as usual but I felt a drift from his usual habits. He would see my messages and then fail to reply. I could see him slipping into the thin air gradually. He would want to meet me every weekend but this time he started to be too busy for that.

I had to respect his decision. Anyway, who does not want to have kids in a marriage worse still marry an ailing wife who will probably die before you enjoy, the fruits of marriage.

One day, he came to my house in much jubilation and I wondered what could be the reason for so much joy

"Cleo I am a happy man today; I got my working VISA and I will be moving to South Africa in the next week" he told me the minute he stepped into my house after over 2 weeks of acting out slow on me.

"Waal, congratulations' I exclaimed. I did not know how to feel or react. This reply had just come out of my mouth without agreement with the entire body system. Henry, had surely decided to leave me with my problems. All this while Henry was processing papers to move to South Africa. He had found work at an engineering company based in South Africa. He never bothered to involve me in the process because I was never part of his plan. Where could an ailing girlfriend fit in, it was actually a scapegoat for him. Maybe he did not want the job offer but he chose to take it so that he would be far away from me.

"This is going to be my last night with you. I will come back after I settle down. I love you my sweetheart, you have to understand the situation in this country. You realize that going abroad is the best thing to do for professionals like us", he tried to explain when he noticed that my mood had suddenly dampened.

He tried to explain that his appointment was facilitated by his nephew who is based in South Africa. His nephew was in the field of civil engineering and had found a job for him which suits his qualification. He is the one who played a leading role in the move. He had bought a one way air ticket for him to board Air Zimbabwe into the neighbouring country. I decided to forget everything and concentrated on bidding farewell to my love. It was probably going to be our last night together. I decided to make it memorable for him. I cooked him a delicious supper of sadza and chicken stew. He had told me how he loved the meal. I made it with all my attention. After all it was our last supper together.

I served the table like never before, made a candle light dinner and I was playing love songs as we ate the food. I could see that the man whom I was never going to make mine was so happy with the food I had prepared. Even though he was going to marry someone else at least he would live with an imagination of what it could have been like if he married me. I was going to miss him anyway. He had chosen a path for himself. A path that would separate him from me without causing me any pain. I respected his decision and resolved to bid him farewell.

Fibroids

As I was picking the plates from the table after eating the presumed last supper a felt a sharp headache that led to extreme dizziness. I could feel a sharp unbearable pain on my lower abdomen. I screamed so loud that Henry was surprised

What is wrong my love". He shouted .

He took the dishes away from me and helped me to sit back on the sofa. This type of pain I had never felt in my life. Tears began to flow down in my eyes as I continued holding my lower abdomen. After 5 or so minutes of great agony the pain vanished and I began feeling normal again. I wondered what was happening as I lay my head on Henry's chest. What started as a romantic dinner had ended in much pain

"Honey, I now feel quite fine do not fret", I told him.

"But you definitely need to see a doctor", he replied.

I agreed to seeing a doctor the next morning. It was a great cramp as if something was moving. I was quite a fragile person now who is affected by all the extreme emotion be it joy or grief. I suffered a stroke at Jakarasi's funeral now I get this on bidding farewell to my love. The whole night Henry could not touch me he was afraid that I would start with that pain again and awaken my landlord. The landlord's daughter Kate had knocked at my door and asked of what was happening the time that I made that scream. If Henry had planned a romantic last night with me all his plans had gone under the bridge because of my health. This is probably what he was running away from. He would play the nursing husband to me the rest of his life.

"Congratulations Cleo you are pregnant", said the doctor when he handed over the results of a urine diagnosis.

"No, doctor it can't be a pregnancy", I replied. How could that be? I am ovarian cancer patient it's not possible. I denied the results vehemently and asked for an ultrasound scan.

I told the doctor about the ovarian cancer diagnosis and the nil possibility of being pregnant because I had not had unprotected sex with my boyfriend. Henry always used protection each time we would have it. The doctor also offered to do another pap smear in order to ascertain the extent of my problem.

Much to his amusement my womb was full of 3 big and grown fibroids and the fourth big mass that looked like an embryo. This brought so much surprise to me. I thought that and so because of fibroids I was going to buy preparation set for nothing. Fibroids are benign non-cancerous tumours that can grow in the uterus or outside the uterus of a female individual. One of them had grown so big that it was the size of a water melon. The doctor suggested we take further tests in order to ascertain several health parameters that might be compromised by the developing condition. They took a blood and urine sample and instructed me to come back the next day.

The results of my diagnosis were very scary I had big fibroid that were eating me up. The fibroids should be treated as a matter of emergency. I needed a blood transfusion too since my blood count has become so low and that was the reason for the stroke-like attacks on me.

I was supposed to tell my grandmother about yet another diagnosis. My grandmother could feel for me, the old lady will practically die if I die before her.

Grandmother, was speechless when I told her about my condition. I told her that I had decided to get the uterus removed. She was of the opinion that I should go ahead if it is safe and she will pray for me to get a successful operation. She had come to terms with the fact that my condition was incurable and it was time to give medicine a chance.

Myomectomy

After several weeks of taking haemoglobin enhancement tablets and eating iron rich food I decided to go for a full treatment at Karanda Mission hospital in Mount Darwin. The mission hospital was popular for treatment of uterus related conditions so I decided to give it a shot. I started on my journey to Karanda.

The journey itself gave me a sigh of relief since I travelled with so much hope and enthusiasm. I arrived at the destination on a Monday evening. On the bus I had made friends with this woman who was going to the hospital for the same condition. It was the second time for that lady therefore she was familiar with the place. We had to look for overnight accommodation at the nearby shopping centre, wake up early for the morning prayer in the chapel and be allocated numbers on the queue.

We woke up early with my newfound friend and entered into the chapel. I looked on as the Chaplain led us in the word of prayer. After the prayer we were given cards with numbers so that we would form a queue to get treatment. My medical aid was not accepted at the mission hospital so I had to pay for everything. I quietly followed the queue to get vital signs assessment and to pay the consultation fee as I eagerly waited for my turn to see the gynaecologist. The white gynaecologist requested another papsmear and ultrasound scan for me. He seemed busy with an operation procedure that he just looked at my results. He was not very amused he only asked me to go and make a decision whether I like to have the uterus removed and then come back with a next of kin if I am ready for the procedure, meanwhile he gave me some iron rich tablets in order to improve my haemoglobin count. He also advised me to get a three months Depo-Provera shot so that I stop mensuration and eventually increase my blood count.

I was confused as i proceeded to the dispensary section to get my medication. I was given a depo shot and moved my legs towards the gate. On this day I never felt any hunger I boarded a lorry that was going to take us to the nearest tarred road in order to get transport to get back to the capital city.

Chido the lady who I had made friends with was also on the lorry. She hesitated before she eventually asked me how it was and what the doctor had said. I had thought I would immediately get a booking for my operation.

Chido then comforted me telling me that it must be a medical procedure to allow the patient to make a decision before they proceed with the operation.

After three months I went back to Karanda Mission hospital. After a thorough visualisation of my vital signs I was put up for myeomectomy.

I signed off the letter of consent to undergo the procedure. "You will be okay Cleopatra do not worry", those were the last words I heard after the anaesthetic specialist had injected me. I began to see faint figures of the operating team as I knocked off.

The procedure took about 3 hours and I eventually woke up. I was the pushed off to the hospital ward where I received medical care for 5 days before I eventually got released to go home and get a full healing.

I was asked to comeback in two weeks and a month later to see if the fissure had healed properly. After 3 months I had completely healed and I was no more suffering from any ailment.

Today I live a happy life. I found love again and I am married to a loving man who has accepted me the way I am and understood me. My grandmother is still proud of me. I am a loving aunt who is adored by her nieces and have a reason to live again.

The End

www.ingramcontent.com/pod-product-compliance
Lightning Source LLC
Chambersburg PA
CBHW021021160726
47994CB00006B/2602